I0531358

Beta Kristoff Dumanovsky has loved his alpha, Jeremiah Tol-liver, for years. However, Jeremiah wasn't ready to move on from the love he still had for his dead wife. When tragedy struck, Kristoff blamed his focus and left not only the Iroquois Pack but Jeremiah as well.

When Stefan Mukhankin, an enemy from Kristoff's past, threatens his safety, Jeremiah uses this as a reason to try to bring Kristoff home. It won't be an easy battle.

Kristoff has survived before and feels he'll survive again. He was trained to elude the enemy, even if it's the man he loves, so Jeremiah is in for the fight of their lives.

Can an alpha help his mate believe their bond is true, or will his mate find yet another place to run?

The unauthorized reproduction or distribution of this copyrighted work is illegal. Criminal copyright infringement, including infringement without monetary gain, is investigated by the FBI and is punishable by up to 5 years in federal prison and a fine of $250,000.

This book is a work of fiction. Names, characters, places, and incidents either are products of the author's imagination or are used fictitiously. Any resemblance to actual events or locales or persons, living or dead, is entirely coincidental.

Broken Promises
Copyright © 2020 Deja Black
ISBN: 978-1-4874-2381-0
Cover art by Martine Jardin

All rights reserved. Except for use in any review, the reproduction or utilization of this work in whole or in part in any form by any electronic, mechanical or other means, now known or hereafter invented, is forbidden without the written permission of the publisher.

Published by eXtasy Books Inc or
Devine Destinies, an imprint of eXtasy Books Inc

Look for us online at:
www.eXtasybooks.com or www.devinedestinies.com

Broken Promises
Broken #2

By

Deja Black

DEDICATION

To my readers who messaged me and asked for the next book.
Thank you for loving my guys.

CHAPTER ONE

Kristoff's trip to the market had been a good one. Mrs. Hilliard would be pleased. The fresh squash and green tomatoes she required for her seafood gumbo were plentiful. After fending off the farmer's daughter's useless flirtations, he had acquired a few other items for himself. He would enjoy Mrs. Hilliard's gumbo, a delicate blend of herbs, spices, and a bevy of crustaceans along with fresh vegetables. Poured over white rice, it was the thing of fantasies. Kristoff pulled the bag tighter against his waist and headed home.

"Thank you, Kristoff. These are perfect. Good color, and" — Mrs. Hilliard lifted the squash and tomatoes to her nose — "perfectly ripe." She hummed appreciatively, then looked up at him, narrowing her eyes. "So, was Jessie there today?"

"Jessie?" Kristoff questioned.

Mrs. Hilliard sighed. "Yes, Kristoff. The farmer's daughter. Was she there?"

Ah, now the trip to the market was beginning to make sense. She was up to it again, trying to find him a mate. Well, it was too late for that. He already had one. A mate he'd left behind with no intention of ever seeing again. It was for the best. He'd already made a mistake once, and it could have cost him the lives of everyone he held close. He wouldn't repeat it.

"She asked me about you the last time I saw her, all bright and sunny, ripe for the picking." Mrs. Hilliard watched him with hope sparkling in her eyes.

1

Mrs. Hilliard was dear to Kristoff. In many ways, she reminded him of Mrs. Dunham, the alpha's caretaker. Mrs. Dunham was like a mother to the pack, keeping secrets, caring for them all, especially Jeremiah. She'd been there when Jeremiah lost Sarai, his mate, and helped to mother Dan and Conner, the children left behind. Kristoff was sure Mrs. Dunham and Mrs. Hilliard would like each other. Mrs. Dunham, too, meddled in her alpha's love life. She'd often hinted that Kristoff should "tell the blind man who can't see the love before him it was there for the taking." But none of that mattered anymore.

When Kristoff had made a choice to go outside his typical mode of operation, to interject himself in such a way to draw attention to only him, everyone important to him could have died. Alonya Romanoff, the bitch who wanted Peter's coven for herself, had seen Kristoff as another way to draw Peter out. It took his nephew getting his wits together and coming to the rescue to save his sorry hide. Something that should never have happened.

He had failed. It wouldn't be the first time, but it would be his last. He had been trained to kill and protect from the age of a child, to never lose focus. He had, and why? Because of a man who couldn't leave his wife's ghost behind. He'd been a fool.

Kristoff leaned back against the counter, sliding his hand along the icy marble. Mrs. Hilliard's husband was responsible for all the work in the kitchen, from the cabinetry to the countertops, to the gray tiled floor on which he stood. He loved the window seat with space for Mrs. Hilliard's well-worn cookbooks below the plush seating. The openness of the room was inviting and housed a massive oven with all the bells and whistles, along with enough nooks and crannies to keep all the tools necessary to create her mouthwatering dishes.

It was work that spoke of love, a testament to the more than forty years the two had shared before a wrong turn on a sharp bend in the road took Mr. Hilliard away. That didn't stop Mrs. Hilliard from trying to help others to find the same love, and Kristoff understood. There was no hope for him, but he appreciated how hard she worked to fill the space where someone to love should be.

"That may well be, Mrs. Hilliard, but I am not the man for her, nor for any other woman. Well, except the divine creature standing before me." His wolf stirred in agitation, but Kristoff urged it to settle.

Mrs. Hilliard's laugh was husky and full, making Kristoff smile.

"Well, I'm still in love with my Rory, so you'll have to make do." She shook her head and turned away from him. Setting the items on the oak wood table, and picking up a knife, she said, "Well, if it's not a woman, then maybe a man? I know a boy or two . . ."

Kristoff didn't need a *boy*. No, what he needed, what he craved with every pull of air into his lungs, was his mate, Jeremiah Tolliver. The thought of his alpha, his mate, pained both him and his wolf. For years, he stood next to the man, serving as his right hand. He'd fought for him, bled for him, because no matter how peaceful nearby packs could be, there were always those who refused to respect the laws that would help all to abide in peace. Many accepted the rules governing the interactions of the different peoples, including the preternatural groups. Yet, as with any society, there were those who didn't follow them. A pack was as mighty and as fruitful as its leader, but that could not exist were it not for those responsible for protecting it.

There was no question of Jeremiah's strength or of his power, which was far-reaching and sometimes even earth-shaking. If Kristoff closed his eyes, he could see the vivid blue

3

eyes of his alpha. His former alpha. On a warm day like this, he'd be wearing a worn thin shirt and walking the compound, Kristoff beside him as it should be.

No, not should be.

Kristoff shook his head, trying to make the image of the breadth and width of Jeremiah's broad shoulders disappear. He needed the ache gathering at the core of his soul to evaporate. Jeremiah's absence made Kristoff feel dead inside. And he knew this was what drove Mrs. Hilliard to help.

"Nothing to say, darling." Mrs. Hilliard's voice pulled him from his reverie. "Wouldn't it be nice to have someone to come home to when work calls you away? Those trips where you return as shadowy as a phantom, and scary to boot, would be better with a person to love you. Such a big house, Kristoff. Even I miss having someone here sometimes, and I enjoy my peace. My Rory's not been gone that long for me to forget what it was like to have a warm body to lay next to. To feel that person's heartbeat so close, it was like we shared the beat itself." She sighed, then turned to look at him. "I'm afraid if you don't let someone in, Kristoff, you'll become the ice you remind me of sometimes."

Kristoff sighed. "I'm fine."

"Yes, darling man, but for how long?"

Kristoff didn't know the answer to that himself.

Kristoff stepped onto his back porch and stopped. His belly was full, and the vessels of gumbo he'd been sent home with permeated the air. He shifted the containers and pressed the buttons to open the door. He loved this house. Even the powder blue color of the building with the white trimming was an aesthetic that appealed to him. The house was two stories and had housed a family or three. It had been used by human families for generations before his sister and her husband purchased it, and the homes nearby were perfect compliments.

Deciding to move near the Charleston Battery had been a great decision, with the park nearby and the beach within walking distance. His wolf missed the hills of Louisville, but there were forests to visit here, where he could allow his wolf freedom. He had to be careful, though. He wouldn't put it past his wolf to try to return to its mate.

And that was not acceptable.

Kristoff prided himself on being in control. Yes, he'd lost his concentration and ended up in the hands of that bitch, Alonya, and almost died. In the end, his nephew had saved not only his mate's life but Kristoff's as well. That had been the reality check he needed. He'd left.

Kristoff didn't mind the emptiness of the home when he entered. Not really. The lack of conversation, items always where he left them? That was what a man like him needed, not adjusting himself to another's temperament. Even if the pain, the loss he felt within was visceral, he would push it away, focusing on the next task or mission ahead.

His last mission had taken him to Istanbul. He loved it there, sitting on the terrace as he enjoyed a meal and the warmth of the Mediterranean climate. If his mind drifted to his former alpha, the movement of the filth that walked below distracted him. His target had been a leader of a criminal outfit that robbed families of their children and placed them in the clutches of the bottom feeders. It had taken him weeks to find Tevrat Yildiz, and killing the man after gaining his connections to others like him had given him pleasure. Kristoff's blade-play on the man's skin, slicing away at him while he remembered the images of those helpless victims, had solidified the ice in his soul. The information he'd acquired went a long way to tracing the locations of the ones who could be saved, and he'd participated in a few of the rescues himself.

When Kristoff had returned home, there was no one to welcome him, to remind him of his purpose. No subtle touches in the dark, like the nearness of Jeremiah when the alpha forgot the wife he still mourned. That moment, summers ago, when Jeremiah had slammed him on his oak desk when he had challenged his alpha was still too vivid an image in his mind to escape. The solidness of Jeremiah's chest, the rigid outline of his cock pressed against his own had stunned him. He'd been too shocked to fight back, or maybe he hadn't fought at all. He could lie to another person, another wolf, but in his head, he was forced to remember the truth, the way he had opened his legs to welcome the length of Jeremiah's powerful form. When Jeremiah had wrapped his open palm around Kristoff's throat and growled, he had yearned with need.

A knock at Jeremiah's door had torn them apart. Still, Kristoff had caught the amber flame blazing in his alpha's eyes, and his panting breaths as if the weight of a hundred freight trains sat on his chest. It was after that moment he'd accepted another mission. He hadn't run, exactly — they'd both needed the separation — but when he returned, Kristoff resolved to keep his distance as much as possible from Jeremiah. And who had he been fooling? Keep away from his alpha, not serve fully in his capacity as beta? It had been a notion absent of reality.

After Alonya, though, he determined it was best he leave the pack altogether. Would he have been caught and beaten by the bitch's man if he hadn't been distracted? Why had he thought going to her, speaking with her, was an option? He had been delusional, a fool.

He shook himself from the past and placed his keys into a porcelain blue and white dish in the entryway, its ring the single sound made.

Turning, Kristoff stiffened when he saw *him*.

"What are you doing here, Jeremiah?"

CHAPTER TWO

Jeremiah had waited impatiently inside Kristoff's house for the man to arrive home. Perhaps standing in his home was outside the rules of common courtesy, but where his mate was concerned, rules of courtesy did not exist. When the door opened, his worries bunched in the pit of his stomach. He was *not* nervous, though. He was the alpha, the absolute ruler of his pack. His word was law.

Except . . .

Except Kristoff had deserted the pack. Apparently, with no intention of ever returning. So here Jeremiah stood, the alpha chasing his beta across states to bring him home.

Mine.

His wolf rumbled with their shared sentiment in his chest, the need to wrap himself around his beta uppermost in his mind, the need to claim the man a tangible thing. But no. Nothing had changed. His soul burned to sink himself inside Kristoff, to show his icy beta who mastered him.

When Kristoff had disappeared, almost a year ago, all had worried, but not Jeremiah. He knew exactly where Kristoff's heart would carry him — to his sister's home, the last that was left of her, his sanctuary. Still, there was something about the city of Charleston, the Holy City on South Carolina's coast, that called to Jeremiah as well. His mate.

Kristoff was no less beautiful than he had been when he'd left the pack. If anything, the absence had only made him more alluring. He wore a dark blue Henley that showed off powerful muscles and accented a narrow waist. Jeremiah vividly remembered tracing those lines with his fingers before — one of the few times he'd allowed himself to touch what his heart wanted more than life but his mind refused to let him have. Kristoff also wore a pair of dark denim pants that outlined his sinewy thighs down to his sandaled feet, which Jeremiah would bend down to lick if given the chance.

The way those grass-green eyes glowed when Kristoff looked at him caused Jeremiah's heart to thrum in his chest. He could tell from the sound of his beta's heartbeat that while Kristoff was shocked to see him, he battled a storm within, a tempest that would not allow him to move toward Jeremiah. Absent was the statement, the promise his beta should have given him the moment he saw him. His lips were pursed as if to trap his tongue.

My arm. Your law.

Words of respect from the pack to its alpha passed from generation to generation. His word was law for Kristoff, or at least it had been.

"This is a beautiful home, *Beta*." Jeremiah deliberately emphasized Kristoff's title, not missing the wolf's flinch at the word. It was apparent Kristoff believed he'd permanently left the pack, but Jeremiah would never allow that to happen.

"I'm no longer your beta, Jeremiah." The words were torn from Kristoff's throat, shredding Jeremiah's soul.

Jeremiah took a deep breath and smiled, but he knew it was brittle. He needed to focus on his reasons for being here. No matter what, Kristoff needed to know how valuable he was to Jeremiah, not just as his beta, or even as his mate. He was Jeremiah's friend, who Jeremiah confided in and trusted with his life and his family. He needed his wolf to know this. All of it.

"That's not a decision for you to make. You know this." Jeremiah looked around, taking in the design of the room, the dark wood that filled the room, and variations of blues in the furniture surrounding him. He admired the plush rugs spread over the hardwood floors and the floor-length windows. "Are you responsible for this? I'd like to see more of your . . . home." He paused before the word and smiled at the flame that lit Kristoff's eyes.

"Not entirely, no," Kristoff said grudgingly. "The seating arrangements were here, but the rugs were additions." Kristoff shook his head slowly. "Fine. Follow me."

They left the living room, walking down a hall broad enough for two wolves to share, then turned the corner into a kitchen that mirrored the one at the compound. Did Kristoff know he'd replicated Mrs. Dunham's kitchen? Jeremiah could maneuver the room blindfolded. The side-by-side commercial-sized expanse of the stainless steel refrigerator shone from one side of the large room with a breakfast nook on the other side. There was an island in the middle, a place where others could gather, as many did in Jeremiah's home.

Jeremiah discretely sniffed the air. Nothing. Inside, his wolf rumbled its satisfaction. No other had been here to spend time with Kristoff, to make Kristoff his own. He hid his smile, not wanting to give himself away.

The windows around the breakfast nook and behind the cooking area provided plenty of light for the room during the day. Yet Jeremiah knew, even without looking, that Kristoff would have installed the same lighting as the compound. It was energy-efficient and hidden within the ceiling, only appearing with a swipe of a hand across a sensor on a wall.

Off to the right, Jeremiah noticed a door to what he assumed must be a large pantry. If it held true to Mrs. Dunham's version, there would be enough food to feed a small contingent of people, perhaps even the entire neighborhood where this house resided. He admired the tiled floor, blue instead of the gold he walked on at home, but the pattern was similar in the way it stretched out. The swirls moved and danced. Jeremiah had to wonder if Kristoff had called Mrs.

Dunham to ensure his measurements were exactly those at home.

"Mrs. Dunham would do well here. It's as if we are in her kitchen now." There were a few items characteristic of Kristoff, a painting here or there, but it was almost an exact copy.

Kristoff nearly moaned at the pleasure he heard in Jeremiah's sigh. The kitchen was hearth to his alpha's home. To know Jeremiah enjoyed what he saw created a happiness in his wolf that could not be ignored. Kristoff often envisioned the two of them together here, sharing a meal, discussing the day, but he never allowed himself to stay in his head for long.

Now, Jeremiah was here.

"We may have spoken once or twice," he revealed.

In truth, Mrs. Dunham called almost daily. The woman never liked her people being too far outside her reach, and according to her, Kristoff still belonged to the pack. She'd asked about his home, the changes, so he'd used his phone to show her. She'd seen the original kitchen and tutted her disproval. Never one to allow the woman he saw as a mother to be disappointed, he'd called that day for a remodeling company and explained in detail what he wanted. It had only taken a couple of weeks to create the exact replica of her kitchen.

And now Jeremiah looked at everything Kristoff had done and was pleased. He had to trap the moan in his lungs, somewhere the alpha would not hear it, but when Jeremiah's eyes lit upon his again, he knew he had failed. Jeremiah stepped forward, but Kristoff cleared his throat and turned, putting away his items from Mrs. Hilliard as his excuse not to look at him.

"I'll show you the rest of the home after I put away these things. If you'll go out—"

"No."

Kristoff sighed, his back still to Jeremiah. "What do you mean, *no?*"

"No, I won't distance myself from you now that you're standing in front of me. No, I won't go back to our home without you. No, I won't leave this room so you can regroup, to deduce a way to get rid of me."

Jeremiah's words spun Kristoff off-kilter. That must have been why he hadn't heard Jeremiah move. Firm hands turned him until they both stared deeply into each other's eyes.

"I won't spend another moment without you." Jeremiah leaned forward, pressing his lips against Kristoff's.

It wasn't the first time Kristoff felt the touch of Jeremiah's lips, or the sweep of his tongue, searing him inside and out. He'd never thought he'd experience it again, though. The first time, Jeremiah had pressed him into a wall, fire blazing in his eyes because Kristoff had challenged him. He had questioned Jeremiah's power over him . . . perhaps baited him. It had been the only way he could get the alpha wolf to see him. He'd come home wearing another man's scent, his clothes saturated with the sweat of another man. He and the human hadn't fucked, but Jeremiah refused to believe it, ripping Kristoff's shirt in two so he could devour him, and Kristoff had done nothing to stop him.

Jeremiah's sharp fangs gliding over his skin, scraping his nipples, was a memory Kristoff would never forget. Then Caleb, the right hand of Peter, Kristoff's nephew, had knocked on the door. Jeremiah had left the room, his clothes disheveled, his breathing heavy and his face flushed.

When Jeremiah had returned, the fire in his eyes was banked, and he was the widowed alpha once again, not the lover of moments before. He'd kept a distance between them after that, though not physically, because the two worked together to care for the pack. Kristoff had accepted it, struggling to let his dreams of being possessed by Jeremiah go. Even so, late at night, he found himself fantasizing about Jeremiah's touch, his own hand strangling his cock before he fell asleep.

And now Jeremiah's hands roamed his body, reaching for the hem of his shirt, touching his skin. Kristoff's wolf ached for this, howling inwardly for his mate.

"Kristoff, so many times I've wanted you, needed you." Jeremiah groaned before he sank his canines into Kristoff's neck.

The fire of Jeremiah's touch created an inferno engulfing Kristoff's senses. He wrapped his arms around Jeremiah's waist, surrendering, submitting to his alpha. It wasn't the mating bite, but it was Jeremiah's mark, and Kristoff's heart was a drumbeat in his chest as Jeremiah shoved him against the countertop, a hand reaching beneath Kristoff's thigh to lift it higher. Kristoff would have given this man anything and everything. He shivered and moaned when Jeremiah growled against his neck, the heat from Jeremiah's mouth teasing the mark on his neck.

Jeremiah lifted him, licking gently at Kristoff's neck. "Forgive me, Kristoff. I would have come sooner. I failed to realize how long it would take you to return to us."

Jeremiah kissed him again, and this time he tasted his own blood on Jeremiah's tongue, following Jeremiah's touch as he backed away. Kristoff sighed when Jeremiah slid his hand down Kristoff's thighs, skating over the ridge of his hard cock.

"I wanted to give you more time," Jeremiah murmured, "but Mukhankin was on his way. I had to warn you."

Jeremiah's words were calm, but they acted like a bucket of ice water dumped on Kristoff's head. Growling, he pushed a surprised Jeremiah back and away. "What did you say?"

Passion still glazed Jeremiah's eyes, the deep red eyes of his wolf just below the surface. But Kristoff could tell Jeremiah was holding back, focusing on his reaction.

Kristoff's wolf struggled within, needing its mate and eager to be closer, back where everything felt so right, but it wasn't. Jeremiah had said a name Kristoff had never forgotten but had always hoped he could.

"Stefan Mukhankin is out of prison and on his way to America. Your former alpha contacted me as your current alpha." He held up a hand to stop Kristoff's retort. "No, Kristoff, no matter what you think or what you've been trying to do, I *am* your alpha. If it takes me bringing you to your knees for you to remember this, I will, but I don't want to, Kristoff. I want you to listen to me. Hear me out."

Kristoff growled, the need to shift close, but he was more afraid his wolf would only settle itself at Jeremiah's feet rather than fight. He wasn't willing to try it and fail. In his wolf's current state, his animal wanted Jeremiah, not only as his alpha but as his mate.

"I'll listen, alpha, but I'll do it in the other room. I'm going to put these things away. We'll talk in the breakfast room. It's down the hall and to the left."

Jeremiah stepped closer. "Kristoff—"

"No, I made a mistake before, and no matter what my wolf thinks, this is a mistake. I was distracted, and people I love, people I promised to shield, were in danger. And, me? I was beaten and nearly killed because Alonya knew about our weaknesses. Now you're mentioning a name I thought time forgot. It can't happen a second time—I won't allow it. And this thing between us can't ever happen."

"Kristoff, I made a mistake." Jeremiah's voice was rough, filled with emotion Kristoff had never thought would be aimed at him.

"No, you were right. I was wrong. Now, please." Kristoff needed a moment, space to get his thoughts together. If Jeremiah wasn't going to leave his home, at least he could leave the room. "The breakfast room is right down the hall and two doors to the left. I'll even make our food, but I need you to leave me be. That's what I need right now. You're my alpha? Well, alphas see to pack needs. Right now, I need you to let me breathe."

Kristoff turned, and Jeremiah waited for a beat before Kristoff heard him walk away.

CHAPTER THREE

Jeremiah sat at a long wooden table, waiting again for the man he heard bustling about to finally make it to the room. He ran his fingers along the surface, the grooves in the wood soothing, the same color as the trees back home on his land. He touched his lips and smiled, remembering Kristoff's submission.

Jeremiah had wasted so much time, too much time. Yes, he'd struggled with the idea of anyone taking the place of his beloved Sarai. But at what cost? He and the wolf he needed in his life were separated. Had been for almost a year because both had been too stupid to acknowledge their need for one another.

It's not too late, my mate.

Jeremiah took a deep breath, deciding to take in his surroundings for distraction. He glanced at the paintings on the wall. One of the pieces, a wolf portrayed in shadow, reminded him of Kristoff's work. He would know his beta's strokes anywhere. He stood to take a closer look. As he got closer, he saw it was two wolves lurking in the shadow, indistinct, yet he noticed the likeness to himself and Kristoff as they stalked prey. The closeness the two shared, the blending of the wolves' movements as if they were of one mind and body, was depicted perfectly in the portrait. Jeremiah had often admired Kristoff's work and was impressed with his ability to capture details so vivid the paintings seem to come to life. Before him was the reality for which he yearned.

He glanced around at the other portraits. One was of a

beach, the ocean waters rolling in, crashing against the shore. There were no wolves there, but it was a lovely painting. Still, his eyes were drawn back to the wolves.

Someday soon, my stubborn mate.

Jeremiah turned to the entryway as Kristoff stepped inside. He could feel the energy rolling off the man, but his beta was his shielded self again. He wore a black fitted t-shirt and a pair of black jeans that left nothing to the imagination. His hair was styled immaculately, giving no indication that Jeremiah had run his fingers through it while devouring him in the kitchen just moments before.

Mmm, my wolf. Seems you feel a need to always be in control.

Kristoff opened his mouth to speak, but words did not emerge. His body tensed when he noticed that Jeremiah was standing near the painting of the wolves. Jeremiah wanted to go to him, tell him how sorry he was for not being there, for not showing him how much he meant to him so many years ago.

"I see you found the room, alpha. If you'd take a seat, we can begin." Kristoff's tone was every bit the professional, no hint of the earlier fire present.

"Kristoff, I want to talk about what happened in the kitchen."

A distinct growl laced Kristoff's words. "A mistake happened, Jeremiah, one I won't repeat. Now Stefan, please." Kristoff was clearly not unaffected no matter how composed he appeared.

This perhaps was not the time to approach him about the kiss, but Jeremiah would see to it that neither of them would forget it. Jeremiah had made mistakes in the past, had ignored his mate, and was paying the price, but he would have Kristoff. For now, he would focus on what Kristoff wanted.

Later, he would get what he came for . . . his mate.

Jeremiah moved to the table and took a seat, his focus never leaving his beta.

Kristoff sat as well, waiting.

"Stefan contacted your former alpha looking for you." Jeremiah started. "He seemed to think there was nothing wrong with this. The way he inquired was like asking for the whereabouts of an old friend."

"He was never truly my friend," Kristoff grumbled.

Jeremiah knew the story. It had been a role Kristoff had played to get what he wanted. Nothing more. When the mission was over, Kristoff had put the man behind bars rather than rid the earth of him. What Stefan knew, according to those Kristoff's family had worked for, was too valuable to lose. They'd wanted him alive, so that was what Kristoff had done. It was an act his mate had regretted for years.

"I know this. I still don't know what happened, or why there is so much pain surrounding this man for you, but the moment I was informed, I came."

"So, that's why you're here." Kristoff nodded as if knowing this could help give him perspective.

"That's not the only reason." Jeremiah then spoke the words he'd wanted to say from the moment he saw his beta. *"You* are why I'm here, Kristoff." He did not want his mate believing otherwise.

Kristoff nodded dismissively, as if the words Jeremiah spoke didn't matter at all. "I need to find out what Stephan wants. Years ago, I wondered if sparing his life had been the best decision. I was young, and he was human. How much damage could he do if left in a cell without means to escape? I thought that if I took out the most valuable piece on the chessboard, there would be no one left. It was what they asked me to do, but I knew it was an idiot move. *Pizdets.* Fuck. It was foolish of me, as it took only days before another vying for power replaced Stefan."

So he would ignore what happened in the kitchen then? Perhaps now was not the time, but there would be later. Jeremiah would make sure of it. He would not give up. On this, he vowed. To have another kiss, to feel Kristoff's body in his hands again, he would do anything, give anything. There was truth to the American adage that absence made the heart grow fonder. There would be no more distance between them, no more absences. Kristoff was his, always had been. Jeremiah had been the fool to think otherwise, wasting all his time wallowing in grief, duty, and stubbornness when he could have shared his heart with a living breathing man.

It wasn't that he didn't still love his wife, his Sarai, who'd lost the battle to cancer so many years ago. He'd loved her with all his soul. She was his mate and had given him two extraordinary sons. Danny Boy, who she'd had with another but was Jeremiah's through and through, and Conner, the next in his line.

Sarai had met every day with happiness, even when her body had turned traitor and her health was failing. When she died, a piece of him went with her. The first years without his mate had been dark ones. He was grateful for Mrs. Dunham, who had stepped in to help him raise his boys when all he could see was his pain. She'd slapped some sense into him, reminded him of his duties to his children and his people, that he was still here . . . alive.

It had taken years for him to realize his heart stirred when he saw Kristoff, that the blood racing in his veins was more robust, so forceful he could hear it. But he'd denied himself and forced Kristoff to back away. There had been times he'd caught the wounded look in his beta's eyes, but he'd ignored it in favor of living as a dying man. Those days were over now. He wanted Kristoff — no, needed him — and he wasn't allowing anything or anyone to take that away, including Kristoff.

"Your former alpha does not know what Stefan wants, why he hunts you. He insisted you be careful." Jeremiah chuckled to himself at the look Kristoff gave him.

Kristoff's silvery brows creased. "I am no fool. Grisha knows this. Stefan was always dangerous, to himself and anyone around him. I should have put him down and didn't. That was my mistake." He sighed. "One I won't make again."

"I don't believe Grisha is worried about your ability to take care of yourself, Kristoff. He mentioned your guilt about the role you played when you approached Stefan, and that years of regret may color your decisions."

Kristoff shook his head. "The only thing I *regret*," he bit out, "is the mistake I made years ago."

"You were young, Kristoff."

"I was foolish. It was a choice I've lived with and wondered if it would bite me in the ass, which it has if Stefan is looking for me. Whatever he wants, it's not to talk."

"How do you know?"

"I don't, and that's the problem. I have no idea." Kristoff looked out toward the window as if searching for something. "He could be here now, waiting for his chance to use a new bag of tools on some poor unsuspecting victim. I should have killed him. Instead, I let him live, and there will be blood on my hands to pay for that." There was a beep. "I warmed up something for us to eat. I'll get it, and something for you to drink, too." Kristoff stood and headed toward the doorway.

Jeremiah smiled. "Thank you, Kristoff."

Kristoff nodded and left the room. When he returned, he placed a plate of meat and pie on the table in front of Jeremiah with a coffee mug. Jeremiah smelled the blackberry currant tea, and his heart swelled. Kristoff's half-smile was knowing, but he said nothing. Instead, he went back to the kitchen, probably to prepare his own meal.

Jeremiah took a sip from the cup and hummed. Blackberry current was his favorite, and Kristoff kept it in his home. On the wall was a portrait of them as they stalked prey painted by Kristoff's hand. He was not foolish enough to think claiming Kristoff would be easy, but there were signs it would not be impossible.

He would take that.

He put the cup down and dug into his meal. When Kristoff returned, Jeremiah was more than halfway done. Kristoff raised a brow, and Jeremiah shrugged. "I was hungry."

"There's more. You can have anything you want."

Jeremiah smiled. "Can I?"

The flush along Kristoff's neck was the only sign his beta had caught the double meaning of his words. He cleared his throat. "Yes, the pantry is stocked and the fridge full. Plenty to eat if you want more food." Kristoff growled, using more force than necessary to dig into his meal.

"I'm staying for a while," Jeremiah said.

"You don't have to stay. I appreciate your coming, but I don't need a babysitter."

"I don't want to be your babysitter, Kristoff."

"Well, you're not here as my alpha. Remember, I left your pack."

You left me. "Kristoff, you left, but you were never alone. Has not a member of my pack contacted you weekly, made certain you were well and safe? Though you refused to give your whereabouts, your inner circle, the few you let in, know where your place of sanctuary is. I allowed you this time and would have given you more had Grisha not called."

Kristoff nodded. "Otherwise, you would never have come."

"No, Kristoff." Jeremiah stared directly into his mate's eyes. "Make no mistake. I was growing tired of your absence. Tired of not having you beside me to lead a pack that has now tripled in size, running over with children and brimming with future possibilities."

Kristoff wiped his mouth and took a drink, turning his

head to avoid Jeremiah's gaze. "Then you should have selected another beta."

"I don't want another beta, Kristoff. The one I need is you. My mate." Jeremiah kept his voice low but firm.

Kristoff growled, shoving his food away, the plates scraping across the table. "Fuck this. You have no right to say this to me, alpha." The title was ground out as if he was chewing on glass. "How many times have I struggled for you to see me? To want me? And the times you did, the times when I finally had your mouth against my throat, your dick trying to shove itself inside me through my jeans, your claws at my waist? You would suddenly remember Sarai, and I would be left aching and alone as you judged yourself, torn and broken and guilt-ridden. And now? Now you want to call me your mate? Fuck you, Jeremiah."

Then he was gone.

CHAPTER FOUR

Kristoff wasn't hungry anymore, he was angry, his rage shoving any fear at learning Stefan was searching for him into the background. Only Jeremiah could make him feel like this. Kristoff had been complimented on his wintry coldness, his ability to stay calm during the wildest moments. He was a man of purpose who didn't have time for dramatic overtures and harlequinesque responses.

His mate.

There was a time when those words would have had him wrapping himself around Jeremiah like a squid and dragging him to the ocean depths of his bedroom. They would have made waves on his California King, and he wouldn't have complained about the disarray, only too happy to offer himself as a sacrifice.

His mate.

He was known for his endurance, his ability to suffer through torture. Before he could make the mistake of going back into the room to beg Jeremiah to take him, he dialed his former pack leader to stave off the insanity. While the phone rang, Kristoff moved to his verandah, a place where he had often felt calm before, where anxiety from his missions evaporated. What he faced here in his home was a battle for his heart. There would be no calm this night. He battled two things from within now. First, feeling so angry he could use the trees surrounding the house as target practice, then being so horny he could use his dick to hammer nails into the floor.

"Hello." The richness of Grisha's accent came through loud

22

and clear.

"Kristoff here," Kristoff said, his voice a shade more emotional than he wanted to reveal.

"Ah, *moy volk*," Grisha said. Even with the distance, hearing Grisha calling him *his wolf* removed the years since they'd last seen each other.

The apparent joy in the voice of Kristoff's former alpha eased some of the tightness in his chest, enough that he could surrender his rigid stand and sit down on one of his rocking chairs. He looked out over the grounds, casting a glance to the neighboring yards, scanning the area for shadows that shouldn't be moving in the dark.

"*Moy volk*, how are you?" Grisha asked.

They shared memories and stories of a time long ago, adding new ones of recent times. The way they spoke was as if they'd just seen each other the day before.

"Congratulations on your mate's pregnancy," Kristoff said. "I am not surprised to hear you are on your fourth pup."

"You are not? Then why am I so surprised?" Grisha's laugh rumbled through the phone.

"Probably because you did not see the possibility of being with a woman who would fight by your side and still have your young."

Grisha had given up on a mate until one arrived who refused to be ignored. In fact, she was all he could see. It was what Kristoff had wanted for himself.

"Perhaps I did not." Grisha sighed. "But it is good. She is good. I am a father as well as an alpha and happy. Though I miss you by my side as I am certain Jeremiah misses you. From what I could tell when he and I last spoke, for him, it is more. What have you done to your alpha, *moy volk*?"

"Nothing."

"Ah, you wish not to tell me, but from the way your words sound, bitter and unsure, I believe there is much to tell. Maybe one day, yes? I am patient. Instead, let's speak of why you have called."

Kristoff settled back in his chair, taking in Grisha's words. Stefan had been miraculously released on good behavior, which should have been an impossibility. Yet with Russia's overcrowded prisons, as well as the corruption existing within, it would make sense. Why someone hadn't looked into his arrests and seen the photos of people Stefan had left behind — disfigured and bloody — Grisha had no idea.

"Too eager to make room for more, and freeing the monsters that needed to stay."

"I should have killed him."

"Yes, you should have, but you did not. This was the fault of the ones who had the power, not yours to hang onto. It is a lesson you have learned and an act that needs to be remedied, which I am sure you will. As the Americans say, you cannot cry over spilled yogurt."

Kristoff smiled wistfully. He had missed Grisha and his inability to capture foreign phrases. He made an effort, but they always came out sounding like the imperfect typing of a fortune cookie message.

"Yes, I will," Kristoff said.

"Good. This is why I contact your alpha." Grisha's tone was unapologetic.

"Not my alpha anymore. I left the pack."

"Kristoff, you, my great wintry wolf, so proud of keeping your feelings wrapped away, unable to be touched by the warmth of love and affection, are not impervious. Your reason for leaving the Iroquois Pack was not fitting, and your alpha has come to return you to your former status and place at his side. From the way he sounded, and his urgency in getting my message to you, he has profound feelings for you. Is that what has made you run, my friend?"

"No. I told you."

"That Alonya captured you and had you beaten when you decided it was best to go into her territory to face her rather than believe your nephew, whom you had trained yourself, could fight this battle? Yes, I remember. And I feel for you and for the nightmares you must have because of this, but it is not your right to deny your mate."

"When he has rejected me again and again?"

"He grieved. The pain of loss makes the vision cloudy at times, Kristoff Dumanovsky. Let us not forget the missions you picked up, the many people you killed because of your sister and her husband's death at the hands of Alonya's people. You waged war against evil on your own rather than allow others to help you, something you would not have done if you weren't as hurt as you were. And now? Now you seek to close yourself off from love, only to have it cross miles to find you."

"He came to warn me," Kristoff insisted.

"*Moy volk*, your safety is not the only thing he wishes to secure. He came for you."

Kristoff kept silent. In the distance, he could hear the laughter of children down the street, a car or two passing by, and the chorus of night. He enjoyed the darkness and used it as a layer of protection when hunting down a target. His wolf's vision was at its best in the dark, able to pinpoint a mouse hiding in the brush while his nose could track its path there. Right now, he allowed the safety of the night to envelope him, to carry the weight of his fears. The trepidation that Stefan would kill the people he loved. Fear that Jeremiah would reject him once again. The terror that he wouldn't be able to keep his shields up long enough to avoid the pain of loving Jeremiah.

"You are quiet, Kristoff. It is no worry. This will come in time. For now, we must focus on the treacherous human that hunts you. When he has been put away . . . Or is it down? Put down, yes? So once this has happened, you will show Jeremiah what he has missed and take your place at his side."

"Grisha," Kristoff warned.

"No, I must go now. If you need my help, I am only a call away. I will come there to America if you need me. For now, allow your mate to do his job and assist you, protect you as he has been doing for years." A baby cried hungrily in the background, followed by Grisha's tender grumbling. He was probably holding his little one. "Yes, yes, little one. The big bad Kristoff is in love and afraid. No, no he won't be stupid enough to let his teeny tiny fears ruin what will be a great union between him and Jeremiah. He's smarter than that. Was that his pride? Oh, that's a part of it, but he'll be smarter and realize he finally has what he wanted all along. Why twist that up? Yes. Oh, little Ava, you are so wise. Such a wise little girl."

"Goodbye, Grisha."

"Goodbye, Kristoff. If you require . . ."

"I will call."

Kristoff ended the call. Grisha's conversation with his little one was not lost on him. He wasn't sure he could trust himself to think about Jeremiah and what they could have. Worry about a future that might never happen for them? No. For now, he would focus on what mattered and allow the other details to take care of themselves.

Kristoff began taking off his clothes. A run would do him good. His sister and her husband had chosen the property for the large forested area behind the house, to afford Lidiya's wolf the freedom it required. Though he missed them both, he was grateful they'd been able to purchase the home even if they hadn't survived to see Peter grow up there. Both had been killed long ago by ancient hate that refused to allow vampire and wolf to mate. Kristoff had inherited the land and his nephew. Lidiya and Alexi Romanoff had known he would keep Peter's safety first in his heart, and he had honored the reason for their decision.

Kristoff welcomed the change as he moved from man to wolf. His palms morphed into pads, claws erupted from his fingertips, and his tail uncurled as he stretched. He shook himself all over as fur covered his entire body. He took in a breath, and his chest expanded until his lungs were filled with the scents of the forest.

CHAPTER FIVE

Jeremiah stood in the shadow and watched as Kristoff prepared to transform. *Mine.* Kristoff was his mate, he knew this. Yet he had failed Kristoff too many times, taking advantage of his need to please, satisfying himself only to leave Kristoff wanting. The guilt weighed heavily on his soul.

Jeremiah realized a part of his soul was lost. He was alive while Sarai, his beautiful love, was dead. Sarai would never have let him wallow in grief this long, but he'd forgotten his way to happiness. He'd merely satisfied himself with the growth of the pack and living vicariously through his sons, Danny and Conner, and his grandchildren.

When Kristoff was not there to talk to, when he no longer had the warmth of his beta's mighty presence at his side, he finally had to accept that he, the alpha who lead so many, had failed not only his pack but himself. They'd lost their beta, and along with that, their direction. They lacked the balance between the alpha and his beta, which had lasted so long it became a necessary familiarity. There were countless times in the past when Kristoff had made the decisions that he had been unable to. Perhaps without realizing it, the two of them had bonded years ago, and he had simply not accepted it. Now, life without Kristoff was no life at all.

Jeremiah watched as Kristoff let his clothes fall, revealing a body hewn from marble, defined and perfect. Yes, there were scars, because no matter how many false stories of their people existed, wolves scarred. Perhaps not as significantly as humans or as permanent, but they did. It felt like it had been forever since Jeremiah had seen them. Among the dips in his skin from bullets of the past, there was a line from a blade down Kristoff's right side. Unfortunately for Kristoff, the weapon had been iron, and it had taken more time than it should to heal the poisoned wound. Alonya had not only meant to kill Kristoff, she'd also wanted his last breaths to be rife with pain.

But Alonya hadn't counted on Jeremiah's ability to heal his pack, the gift of the alpha who was both protector and provider to his people. He had worked diligently on easing Kristoff's pain, catching glimpses of his mind as he sent his spirit within. Kristoff was tenacious, though, and refused him entry several times, which made the healing process last even longer. To heal, Jeremiah had to connect, and with Kristoff blocking him again and again, the process had been slow. Jeremiah should have taken that as a sign Kristoff had planned to run. Because the moment Jeremiah had noticed his beta was aggressive enough to rise against him, he disappeared.

I screwed up once. Never again.

When Kristoff stood naked, the moonlight hit his skin, and Jeremiah's mouth watered, his teeth dropping with the desire to mark his mate, to finally claim him. Before he could move, though, he regained his control, taking several deep breaths. It would not do to go to Kristoff as a mate who hungered when Jeremiah had denied him so many times before. No, he would take the time needed to show Kristoff he could be counted on, that he was worthy.

Kristoff was a beautiful man, with or without clothes. He'd allowed his platinum blond hair to grow beyond the military cut he usually wore. It gave him a relaxed look, one that had quickly disappeared the moment he realized Jeremiah was in his home. Fur raced over Kristoff's body, covering him entirely, leaving none of his human flesh visible. His wolf was stunning in size and breadth, his silvery pelt catching the light from the moon. He dropped to the ground, much larger than any gray wolf. He was massive and worthy of respect. Kristoff shook, and the moonlight shimmered along his body, reflecting in the fur. One deep breath. Two. Then, his beta was off, charging into the night.

Kristoff ran, his panting loud to his own ears. He was aware of the animals nearby if he chose to hunt. Kristoff loved the home and the land on which it sat. He often took advantage of the forest, the aroma of the trees and wet grass helped to clear his mind.

He dodged fallen logs and leaped over branches and inhaled the scent of small creatures like the predator he was. And he continued to run. His goal had been to rid Jeremiah from his mind, but his smell was everywhere, permeating his flesh, his lips remembering the voracious kiss they'd shared earlier. He would be lying to himself if he thought he didn't want what Jeremiah appeared to be offering. It was something he had dreamed of for years.

Perhaps I have what I've wanted since the first moment I saw him? But how long before Jeremiah snatches the dream away, leaving me broken and lost.

A hint of white stopped, freezing in place, but Kristoff wasn't interested in rabbits, or the red fox quivering in the brush. What he wanted to do was escape, if only for a moment.

He ran.

Jeremiah had allowed him time, a head-start before he gave chase. He stripped out of his clothes, peeling the Henley from his body, pushing the jeans he wore down his thighs, leaving his clothing and shoes in the mudroom. Padding across the room on naked feet, he opened the door.

The night air was magnificent. No, it wasn't his home in Louisville, Kentucky, the territory he'd grown fond of over the years. The land there supported his pack, and he lovingly nurtured it to bolster the steady growth they experienced. There he knew every spot, every hidden nook. Here was foreign to him, a bevy of unknowns, but he was a wolf. This land was a forest. And more importantly, his mate was out there.

Jeremiah allowed the change to overtake him, the rush to race into the night, propelling the switch to occur faster. In moments, he stood on four legs, muzzle lifted high as he scented the air for his mate. There, the scent of musk on the air along with sandalwood and traces of ginger, Kristoff. He'd given his mate enough time alone. He raced off in pursuit of what was his.

As a wolf, Jeremiah was still aware of the man within, but he was more. The night opened before him, the light of the moon, the only illumination he needed. He relied on his instinct, his baser half, whose focus was on finding their mate. He ran over roots and past trees, ignored the hint of a quivering rabbit and the small mice within the brush. He was a streak of black hidden in the depths of the forest as he hunted, eager, and ready.

Kristoff's scent was near, so Jeremiah slowed until he spotted him standing near a lake, pacing as if in thought. Jeremiah crouched low, his belly barely touching the forest ground. He saw the moment Kristoff realized he was near. His beta's muscles tensed, and he moved closer to the water's edge to increase the distance between them. Jeremiah growled his displeasure and moved closer. Kristoff might have been able to reject him in his human form, but for the wolf, it would be nearly impossible not to be near his mate. Jeremiah was counting on that.

He barked and smiled internally at the way Kristoff's ears perked up. Kristoff let out a low growl before once again moving away, this time turning to face him. Jeremiah shook his head, an indication of his displeasure at Kristoff's distance.

Kristoff bowed his head and began inching closer to him.

Slowly, carefully, Kristoff notched his head beneath Jeremiah's, allowing him the room he needed to curve himself over Kristoff protectively.

His mate.

Jeremiah's mate needed him, was close to him. He breathed in the scent of Kristoff's wolf and allowed himself to be satisfied with Kristoff's nearness. He pressed himself against Kristoff until his beta sat on the forest ground. Jeremiah wrapped himself around Kristoff's large frame, and they lay together content, the sounds of the forest surrounding them. Kristoff's labored breathing became calm, and he slept while Jeremiah watched over him, now and then rubbing his muzzle possessively over Kristoff's.

Eventually, Jeremiah nodded off as well.

The first time he heard the screams, he imagined they were in his dreams. He twisted and turned, searching for the source. The next time the cries reached his ears, he was fully awake. Kristoff moved beneath him, his body alert. They both shifted quickly and ran back toward Kristoff's home.

"My clothes!" Kristoff shouted.

"Of course, and mine, too," Jeremiah called back. They both arrived at the door of Kristoff's home and were dressed in seconds.

The scream came again. "Mrs. Hilliard!" Kristoff took off.

At the look on Kristoff's face, Jeremiah's blood ran cold. He followed Kristoff as they ran off in the direction of Kristoff's next-door neighbor.

The fear that rose off Kristoff's flesh was a clear indication he'd developed a relationship with his neighbor. Jeremiah hoped all was well, because Kristoff didn't need any other feelings of guilt weighing on his heart. It would make it that much harder to get him back to Louisville, where he belonged.

When they arrived at the house, there were flashing lights. Police cars were scattered on the streets and sidewalks, waiting for their owners to return. Kristoff continued past them, his strides intent and purposeful.

"Mrs. Hilliard!" Kristoff's powerful baritone rang over the noise, causing a head or two popping up to discover the source.

Jeremiah's instincts immediately kicked in, his need to stake his claim so all looking would see Kristoff was his. In time. The moment was inopportune, but they would get there. He would make sure of it.

"Kristoff. Oh, goodness. Please let him through. They think I'm a crazy woman, boy. And I know what I saw. I know, Kristoff." A raging inferno fueled those words, a spirit Jeremiah admired immediately without even seeing the owner of the voice.

"Ma'am," a placating voice said laced with humor, which grated on Jeremiah's nerves.

"Don't you ma'am me. I told you to let my boy back here. You won't listen to me, so I don't care what you want. The lot of you can get out of my house, off my yard, and go home. I have people. You're not them."

Her voice rose louder in irritation, and if they could get around the officer standing in front of them, it would make life easier.

"I'm coming, Mrs. Hilliard, as soon as the officer moves aside," Kristoff said through clenched teeth. "Or as soon as I move him."

The uniformed officer's eyes drew tight, and he pressed his hand to his side, which Jeremiah saw as a move to reveal his weapon.

"Is that a threat," the officer asked.

"Charlie, let him through. We're done here. Ma'am, if you see the perpetrator again, be certain to let your neighborhood watch know. Even with us being in the area, I can't promise we'll be here that quickly the next time you see a man who can change into a wolf."

Imagine the luck. Stefan was free, and now his quarry was in sight. He'd been waiting years to see Kristoff, and there across the street, the man himself stood, blocked by a tiny gnat of a police officer. The officer's goal was obviously to bar the wolf from entering the house. It was all silly posturing, really, because what could the officer do against someone as mighty as Kristoff Dumanovsky?

"Do you want me to get him?"

"No, you've drawn enough attention, don't you think?" Stefan said. "I just needed you to bring him running, which you did. Now, let's stand back and watch the entertainment."

"We could kill him. Him, and the other one." The foolish wolf's voice filled with eagerness.

"No, we won't be doing that. Touch one hair on the silver-haired one, and your gang loses a wolf. He's mine. We have a destiny, he and I."

The wolf standing at his side huffed. "As if you could do a thing to me, human. The only thing we need from you is your money. After that, you can fuck off."

Stefan quickly pulled a blade from inside his jacket and slashed it across the wolf's neck. He'd been assured when he purchased it that the metal was solid iron. It would be one of the items he'd use to help Kristoff see clearly. It was a shame he'd had to baptize it with the fucking stupid wolf's blood first.

"You can't do this." The wolf's words were garbled already, his throat unable to heal with Stefan's foot pressing against it, cutting off any silly words he might deem to spew.

"You think I came all this way for your threats. You think

I chose your pitiful gang of wandering wolves idly. No, dumbass. Where are they now? No one came with you, had your back. Your group lacks that great pack loyalty I've heard about. They let you travel alone with a human they perceived as weak. Had you been an actual pack, you lying on the ground bleeding to death would never have happened. Good for me, dire for you." Stefan pressed harder. "This is taking too much time." He looked across the streets and noticed the cars leaving. "You need to die faster so I can check on my wolf. He needs me. You will only be a memory."

Stefan shoved the blade deep into the wolf's chest and twisted. Taking another from his boot, he opened the dying wolf's neck wider, slashing his skin in choice places that would bleed the wolf out. He left the carcass as a treasure for the vermin in the shadows. "There. What is of the earth will now return to the earth."

Stefan wiped off his hands and walked away, focused on seeing as much as he could of his beloved friend's reaction. A few sizeable breadcrumbs should lead Kristoff to him. It would make the dance more fun, the pleasure at the end worth drawing out the foreplay. Every love affair he'd read about while behind the bars where Kristoff had left him had taught him the importance of foreplay, romance, and how using them would help add fire to their relationship. Stephan wanted a blaze.

The grass was wet as it bent beneath his steps, another sign of the early hours of the day. Stefan breathed deeply, and the smile he wore filled with happiness. His day was off to a great start.

He neared the home of the old woman, observing the way some officers packed quickly and sped off while others hung around, glancing back at the house.

"Crazy old woman," one of the officers said. The man shook his head while striking the bottom of a cigarette box.

When he'd retrieved one of his cancer sticks, he used a flame from an offered lighter to bring the end to life. "Someone needs to do a wellness check here. She has a nice house, nice car, and it seems like a family that cares. Why's she out here alone?"

"That's what happens, Pat. You live for so long you become vulnerable to your mind. She's a tough one, more lucid than you give her credit. Maybe she did see something."

"Yeah, Tick, a man changed into a wolf in her home while a guy asked questions about who she knew in the area, threatened her about what she didn't know about monsters in the world while tossing a blade from hand to hand. That happened. That shit's right out of a movie. No fucking way."

The taller officer—Tick, Stefan assumed—laughed nervously. The man knew something, knew about things most did not, or refused to acknowledge. Stefan would lay money down. He waited, but Tick patted his partner's shoulder and eased him toward the car. "No, you're right. She saw things. A wellness check would be a great idea. I think I'll drop by tomorrow."

"Yeah, like you don't already do for half of Charleston. What's another person to you, right? Maybe I'll come with you."

There was that flicker of alarm again. Tick coughed. "No, man. It's no trouble. She reminds me of my aunt, you know? Someone who needs watching."

"Your aunt, huh?"

Their voices trailed off as they split up, opening the doors to their police vehicles and climbing in.

Stefan crept nearer to the house, wanting to catch an actual glimpse of Kristoff. It had been so long since he'd seen the man—the wolf—who had stood tall and deadly on the line between life and death. The ability to take Stefan's life had been in the palm of Kristoff's hand, but he hadn't. He'd chosen to allow Stefan to live. Placed him in a prison where none could attack him.

Stefan had had no idea the vines of defection that twisted through his organization. He had been surprised when word had made it to him of the ones who'd taken leadership only to be killed by others vying for their turn at his seat of power.

It could have been him killed, would have been him. But Kristoff had saved him.

And then Stephan had met Malik, a man who had told him about men who could change into wolves. At first, he'd ignored the man. He'd had better things to focus on, like what he would need to do to get out of the cage. But the guy had kept talking, kept sharing his stories, until something he'd said caught Stefan's attention. Stefan had looked up then, his eyes settling on the other prisoner across from him. Things came together in a way that oddly made sense. Destiny.

"Kristoff. That's the one that got you locked up in here." Malik had said. "One day someone's going to get him, put him behind these bars, might even take some iron to his chest and end him. He won't come for anyone else. You know?"

Stefan had finished sorting the laundry as plans filtered through his mind. It had been so easy for him to snap Malik's neck for a quick death, the skin supple beneath his grip. Since he and Malik had been considered safe, the lack of a guard nearby was a boon. He pushed the basket with Malik wrapped in the sheets toward the door and into a room where he wouldn't be discovered until the next morning, no longer able to spread secrets.

As for Stefan, he had a purpose now. Save Kristoff from himself. Show him what he could become. Kristoff was a wolf who deserved a pack, who needed to lead. Stefan could be the first human alpha of a pack that belonged to someone who deserved it. No, it wouldn't work no matter how much he wanted it. He would have to give that title to Kristoff. Then he could use that power for himself. To accomplish this, Stefan would have to break Kristoff down, show him who he could be, where he could be safe. Show him Stefan was his only sanctuary.

Stefan had kept feelers out for anything involving Kristoff. He knew about Jeremiah, the alpha, the supposed leader of the pack in Louisville, Kentucky. He didn't know what determined who became the boss, but it couldn't be different than his former organization. He assumed Jeremiah was like he had been before Kristoff had realized the danger he was in and rescued him. Kristoff had given him the time to rebuild his resources. He was now ready to make his move.

After learning what Kristoff was, Stefan had discovered his purpose. Kristoff needed him, a person at his side who could strengthen him. The photos he'd seen of Kristoff and Jeremiah together revealed Kristoff's misguided feelings for the alpha. Others probably lacked the ability to see, those who weren't as appreciative of details and missed the heightened desire for Jeremiah that Kristoff laid bare only for him to see.

Kristoff was worthy of someone who prized him. It was Stefan's fortune that Jeremiah failed to realize the gift he held in his possession. Stefan knew Kristoff's value and wanted him, even if he didn't want to fuck him. Of course, he wasn't above accepting a blow job from Kristoff — those lips wrapped tightly around his cock as Kristoff sucked him dry. If Kristoff wanted him to use his hole, he could do it. He'd had practice with plenty of guys begging for it while locked away. Stefan wouldn't hesitate to offer whatever Kristoff needed to help him attain the position they both deserved.

Sustain the alpha and acquire the role of authority in Kristoff's pack, one that would ensure he played a part in decision making. In time, Stefan would have more money than he dreamed and never be in danger again.

There would be times when he'd have to fuck women, though. Like that pretty little thing the wolves kept hidden away from him. His preferences for tender flesh weren't as hidden as he thought.

He could pretend Kristoff's ass was her pussy, and he'd fill him with his seed in no time.

Stefan quietly eased around the corner of the house. The homes in the neighborhood were brightly colored, nothing like the gray on gray brick and desolation that had surrounded him in Russia. It wasn't difficult to travel unnoticed when the rainbow color scheme of the houses served as the backdrop. It hadn't taken much to gain entry through the woman's doors and then into her kitchen. Her look of terror when his accomplice had fallen to his knees as a wolf was charming. He'd thought of teasing her skin with the blade he carried but was able to resist, barely. There was something about a knife as it pierced the skin, opening the life source, that tempted Stefan as nothing else did.

But he wasn't there to kill the woman, only shake her faith in her next-door neighbor, instill a little fear. Destroy Kristoff's world.

It would be the first step of many he would take as he directed his future alpha's path.

Make him need. Make him bleed. Make him desperate.

Then Stefan would return the favor. He would save Kristoff because he needed to be saved. Kristoff just didn't know it.

CHAPTER SIX

Kristoff placed his hand at Mrs. Hilliard's back, guiding her toward the back room where she liked to sit. Her home was similar to his, large enough for two families to live, a stairway as the focal point of the architecture. There was a study at the back of the home that boasted a vast library of books he borrowed from occasionally. He pulled the string for the lamp and helped a woman he loved deeply settle into her favorite chair, the one she often relaxed in when he visited. He tossed a bevy of pillows from the chair he took for himself and pulled it close. Taking her soft hand is his, he listened as she complained about the officers and the way they ignored her.

"Would you like some tea, Mrs. Hilliard," Jeremiah asked in a calming tone, his accent deepening his voice and teasing Kristoff's dick to a metal rod in his pants.

The moment was surreal. Here his alpha—no, his former alpha—stood in the home of his neighborhood friend, asking her if she needed tea. He shook his head.

"And who might you be, young man?"

Kristoff snorted. *Young.* Though Jeremiah didn't look it, he was more than twice Mrs. Hilliard's age. One would never know from the thickness of those black locks, the hard muscles decorating his tall frame, and the way he glided with every step, his wolf ever-present.

"My name is Jeremiah, and I am a friend of Kristoff's."

"Friend, eh? I've never heard my boy speak of you. Keeping more secrets, then, Kristoff?" Her sharp gray glare captured Kristoff's attention.

"Life would be boring if there weren't a few secrets to keep, my lady." The woman's howl of laughter warmed Kristoff inside.

"Tea, Jeremiah. Yes, I'll have that. You'll find my home very similar to your *friend's*. My favorite would be the sassafras root one to the left of the microwave. You bring me a cup of that, and I'll sit here and enjoy Kristoff's company a bit." She returned her attention to him once Jeremiah had left to do her bidding. "Friend. Hm. The way he looks at you, any fool can see it's more than a friend he's wanting . . . or thinking, boy."

"That's all that can be on the table," Kristoff whispered.

"For now?"

Kristoff shook his head. "Stop prying, woman." He released her hand and stood to pull a blanket from the love seat. Placing it over her lap and kissing her temple. "I'm not interested in anything further."

"Ah, seems you're keeping a few secrets from yourself as well. Because I am not blind to the way your eyes search for him."

"I never fail to appreciate your skills of observation, but can we leave it for now? It's a long story, and not one I'm interested in sharing. There are too many variables, too many memories casting the possibility of more in the shadows."

"Son, nothing's stopping the two of you from bringing that possibility into the light if you truly wanted it," she said gently.

Kristoff glanced toward the kitchen, hearing Jeremiah maneuvering about. He sighed. "Some things are just not meant to be." He turned back to her with a wan smile, trying to ignore the pain in his heart.

Just when he'd finally stopped pining for his alpha — no

longer hungering from afar or acting satisfied with whatever tidbits of affection Jeremiah cast his way—the man showed up in his house. When this was over, he'd probably have to throw himself into a mission to get his head back on straight. Even now, he struggled with his wolf seeking his mate, the desire to be near Jeremiah causing turmoil within his soul.

"Are you sure you want to stay here tonight?" he asked Mrs. Hilliard. "You could stay with me."

"You've already asked me this, and I told you I would stay here. Now, my daughter should be here in a couple of hours. She's been threatening to have me move in with her, and I think after today, I'm open to considering it. When a man changes into a wolf right before your eyes, you have to question your sanity." She shook her head. "I swear it was real, Kristoff. I promise you it wasn't the effects of a prescription or too little sleep."

Kristoff wanted nothing more than to remove Mrs. Hilliard's self-doubt. But sharing with her would only place her in more danger.

Jeremiah sighed as he entered the room. "Who can say what exists beyond man's perception? There are so many layers to this world. I hope this will soothe your spirit, Mrs. Hilliard." He bent low to hand the woman the tea, and the smile she granted him was both kind and suspicious.

"Thank you, Jeremiah. While that is true, I'd rather not be the one accused of having flights of fancy. For almost ninety, I've been so proud of my clarity in my old age. To have someone blame what I witnessed happen in my kitchen on an addled mind, or some type of delayed reaction to some medication, makes me angry as a squid cheated out its supper. I need to know, and what's peculiar is I feel you two know something and are leaving this old lady in the dark." Mrs. Hilliard leaned back, her lips at the rim of the cup as she blew across it while carefully holding it with both hands. Slowly she took a sip and smiled. "That's nice. I do love that flavor." She sighed and rocked, contemplating Jeremiah. "Tell me a little about yourself, Jeremiah."

"Well," Jeremiah said before taking a seat. "I run a business in Louisville, one that's taken care of my large family for years."

Centuries. Kristoff barely held back a snicker.

"Oh, and what would that be?" She was meddlesome, his Mrs. Hilliard. Kristoff reflected on her encounter while she and Jeremiah chatted as if her life hadn't been threatened earlier.

"Furniture. Custom made pieces, more specifically. That was where we started, but with the addition of new members, we moved into different fields. Among them security, a chain of stores, and even stores catering to animals, which my son Conner's wife handles."

"So, you have children, then?"

"I have two sons, Daniel and Conner."

"And is there a wife at home waiting for her husband's return?" Mrs. Hilliard's eyes were sharp as she watched Jeremiah.

"No, no wife. My beloved Sarai died many years ago. It took me some time to let her go, but I realize now she would have wanted me happy, not married to a ghost. She would have wanted me to live again."

Kristoff could barely breathe. Jeremiah's words squeezed his lungs, making it difficult to get air through. He felt Jeremiah's stare, but he refused to return the look, refused to hope.

"Ah, it takes time to grieve when you've shared a life with someone, and we have to be ready in our own time. It's not a thing that can be forced or hurried." She reached out then and touched Kristoff's hand. "Would you mind getting me a glass of water, Kristoff?"

"No, not at all." He stood and appreciated the reprieve. The longer he remained in the room with Jeremiah, the more the need to submit grew. He was physically aware of the man's presence in ways he hadn't been for a while. He wanted Jeremiah, wanted to touch him, to taste him, and his words about moving on, about living again, did not make it any easier.

When he returned with the glass, it was to hear Mrs. Hilliard ask, "How long are you staying, Jeremiah?"

There was a purpose behind her questions. Kristoff could see it in the way she observed Jeremiah. As for Kristoff, he wanted to do more than observe. He was tempted to lie on the floor with his ass in the air and wave it like a target directing his mate home. The barrage of heat flowing over his skin had nothing to do with the warmth in Mrs. Hillard's house, and more to do with being in the same room with Jeremiah.

In the past, he'd grown accustomed to Jeremiah's presence, and while the need to have him was never absent, it was at least easier to manage. Now, with so much time having passed, Jeremiah's scent was overwhelming, and his body ached for more of the touches they'd shared earlier. He felt like a man who'd discovered water when stranded in the desert.

Jeremiah looked at him then, a knowing curve to his lips. "As long as it takes."

Kristoff and Jeremiah were quiet when they walked into Kristoff's home, or the place he'd called home for almost a year now.

"Kristoff, we need to talk about what happened at your friend's house."

Kristoff nodded. They had both stayed until Mrs. Hilliard's daughter had arrived to pick her up. She'd been grateful to them for keeping Mrs. Hilliard company, but the look in her eyes as she watched her mother indicated just how worried she'd been. They packed what she would need for a weekend stay, tabling a discussion of a more permanent move for when Mrs. Hilliard was ready.

Mrs. Hilliard told them to be careful, that she had a *feeling*. Then she'd leaned into Kristoff to whisper where she kept a drawer of condoms in her bedroom. He had blanched, while Jeremiah had laughed out loud.

"Never too old for a little fun, I say." She winked, then allowed Kristoff to help her into the car.

Kristoff now stood in the foyer of his too-quiet house, where he could hear not only the thumping of his own heart but that of Jeremiah's as well. When he felt Jeremiah move toward him, he slid away, out of reach, and turned. "I'll get you a room ready, and we can talk in the morning." He deliberately faced away from him, unable to look at the man who'd turned his world upside down again.

"Kristoff?" Jeremiah was closer now, his breath teasing against Kristoff's ear, making him tremble.

"Not now. I . . . not now. I need a little distance." He wouldn't be able to handle his heart being broken again. The loss would be too much once Jeremiah realized Kristoff wasn't who he wanted regardless of the bond they'd shared for years. Sarai's ghost, the memories of what she and Jeremiah had shared, would come between them again, leaving Kristoff with nothing.

"You've already had your distance. Months of distance. Let me be near you." Jeremiah wrapped his hand around his waist, pulling him against him, his back to Jeremiah's broad chest.

Kristoff could feel the twin beatings of their hearts, but it was a symphony he sought to ignore. "Why, Jeremiah? Why now? For so many years I struggled. I can't." Jeremiah's lips were at his nape now, the press of his sharp teeth nipping at his flesh.

"I know, Kristoff, and for that I'm sorry. But I won't waste another moment. I won't be chased away. You need me, and even if you don't want to believe it, I need you. So I'm staying until we leave and you're with me." The words were a growl.

Kristoff moaned when Jeremiah turned him around and then stepped into him, both hands spanning his chest, sliding over his hungry skin. Jeremiah's leg pushed between his thighs, hands reaching beneath his shirt, and the bliss of having what he'd wanted forever nearly broke his control.

"Mine. I was too blind to see it, too stupid, and I let you go. Not again, Kristoff. My beta. My mate. Fucking mine." Jeremiah's kiss was violent, a storm with the force of a typhoon as Kristoff's head slammed against the wall, Jeremiah's lips crashing over his.

Kristoff could no longer ignore his need. He spread his legs to give Jeremiah room as his alpha slid a hand down the front of his body over the ridges of his waist and down to the buckle of his belt.

Jeremiah pulled the belt roughly until it was loose and he was able to reach underneath the fabric to wrap his questing hand around Kristoff's leaking cock. Kristoff opened his mouth to cry out, and Jeremiah dipped his tongue deeper, growling as he nudged at Kristoff's flesh. Kristoff fucked his hand, moaning and whimpering shamelessly.

"So long. Waited so long to do this, to see you come apart beneath my hands." Jeremiah's voice a hot whisper against his ear.

"Jeremiah. Gods. Jeremiah."

"Beautiful mate. My beta. My love. I'm so sorry I failed you, but I have you now. Never leaving you again."

Tears slid down Kristoff's cheeks. He'd dreamed of this too many times, hoped for Jeremiah's touch, his words. Prayed, even. Maybe now was a dream, and he would awaken from this broken as he had so many times before.

"No, Kristoff. Not a dream. Let me prove it to you."

Had he said the words aloud? He had a second to wonder before Jeremiah pulled his pants down his thighs. Then his dick was encased in a wet heat so precious he shouted his pleasure for the world to hear.

It was too much and not enough. Kristoff thrust forward into Jeremiah's mouth and trembled with the vibration of Jeremiah's moan.

"Please, Jeremiah. Please." Kristoff was a begging, whimpering mess. How many enemies had he brought down, battles had he fought, injuries had he suffered and overcome? Yet here he stood at the mercy of the man who was sucking his brains out. He opened his eyes and looked down to see Jeremiah watching him, his eyes red with his wolf present, his lips stretched wide around his dick.

Kristoff watched mesmerized as Jeremiah took one of his fingers and slid it between his lips and Kristoff's cock. He shook when that finger, that dangerous digit, skated over the surface of his hip and around to the curve of his ass. His cheek was pulled aside, and without preamble, Jeremiah shoved his finger into Kristoff's ass. Then Jeremiah opened his throat wider as he forced another finger into Kristoff's ass.

"Shit. Right there. Right fucking there. Oh, Goddess. That's it. Fuck. That's it." One touch, one press against that fucking amazing ball of nerves inside Kristoff, and he shot off like a rocket, his cum greedily swallowed by the man who had demolished him, body and soul.

Kristoff slid down the wall and into Jeremiah's waiting arms.

"Mine," Jeremiah growled before he kissed him, sharing the flavor of his seed. "Next time, it's going to be my dick in your sweet ass."

Kristoff moaned weakly, too gone to answer. Or maybe that was all the answer Jeremiah needed.

CHAPTER SEVEN

Jeremiah yawned as he stretched out his arms. He hadn't liked the idea of leaving Kristoff to sleep in a separate room, but he needed to give the man time to accept him fully. Jeremiah couldn't rush Kristoff. He needed to show his mate this was the forever love he'd offered Jeremiah so many times in the past. He would be a fool to expect Kristoff to drop everything and allow another to protect him for a change, to have his back. To have him.

No, he would be patient, as patient as he could before the wolf in him decided enough was enough and he claimed his mate on the floor. Thinking about his dick sinking within the delicious warmth his fingers had only teased the night before made him shudder. Kristoff's scent was still on his body, the flavor of his seed still on his tongue. He wanted more, but first, he needed a shower.

"Up and at it, wolf mine. Let's go and find our mate, yes?" His wolf huffed, so eager it nearly howled.

Refreshed, Jeremiah entered the kitchen and smiled when he saw Kristoff at the stove. "You're cooking."

"Yes. I have to eat, and I don't have a chef or anyone to fix my meals like some wolves. Learning how to cook was necessary if I want to ensure what I eat doesn't kill me." The smell of eggs and bacon wafted through the room. "Besides, Mrs. Hillard's been rather insistent about making sure I'm fed, even if I say *no*." The thin line of worry lacing Kristoff's words drew Jeremiah close to him.

Jeremiah hadn't wanted to force things by insisting he

share Kristoff's bed. That was a sure way to make the man balk. But if he eased his way in, showed Kristoff he was there for the long haul, perhaps his mate would have more faith in him. It was difficult. He was an alpha, after all, accustomed to having his way, to his word being law and undisputed. Here, he would have to tread carefully. Kristoff was able to live life on his terms, and Jeremiah wanted that life to be with him. "It smells good."

The small smile Kristoff displayed was Christmas and New Year's Day for Jeremiah. It was the sun on a brutal Kentucky winter day. It was a hint of the *more* he could have, and a prelude to all he ever wanted.

"Good. I made enough for both of us. We'll sit and talk while we eat, make plans for our approach."

Yes, because neither of them could forget the danger that existed. A man and a wolf had entered Kristoff's domain. It did not matter that it wasn't his home. It was his territory, and Mrs. Hilliard belonged to him. Since she was Kristoff's, she was also Jeremiah's and would be protected as such.

No matter what Kristoff believed or struggled against, he was still Jeremiah's.

"Plates?" he asked.

Kristoff raised a silver brow before cocking his head to the cabinet on the right above the counter. "There." He turned back to the stove and pulled the oven door open. "Biscuits are almost ready. If you want jelly or honey, I have both. I did some shopping the other day when I got back."

Jeremiah walked to the cabinet and opened the door, pulling two plates from the shelf. He noticed how very similar they were to plates his own Mrs. Dunham used in her kitchen at the compound in Kentucky. Perhaps Kristoff didn't realize he had recreated the home he'd shared with Jeremiah for so many years.

Now all Jeremiah had to do was convince the man that

home was with him. After they'd gotten rid of the evil in between.

They sat together, digging into the breakfast. Kristoff was a beautiful man, always had been. He was the light of the moon with his silvery hair. Jeremiah enjoyed watching Kristoff's fingers flex around the fork, envisioning that hand wrapped around his cock instead. He found himself flashing back to the previous night when he'd swallowed Kristoff's hard dick. He licked his lips and nearly growled when Kristoff's gaze flickered to him and away.

"We need to talk."

"Aye, that we do."

Kristoff's shoulders relaxed. "Your Irish is showing."

Yes, he'd caught himself. Sometimes it could not be helped. He'd lived more than a hundred years here in America, but the language of his homeland still came through occasionally. The accent was even greater when he was losing control of his wolf and the outward appearance of calm he worked diligently to maintain. The need to have Kristoff acknowledge him as mate rumbled through him, but that simply couldn't be the focus right now.

Right now, they had to figure out Stefan's motives, what he was after. There would be time to claim his mate. "Sometimes I can't hide it."

"Well, there are things you certainly can."

"Kristoff . . ."

"No, Jeremiah. Not now. Last night was . . . Fuck. Last night was a mistake. One I don't wish to repeat."

Jeremiah had done this. He'd had so many chances and opportunities to acknowledge his mate, but he'd put him in a box, labeled him as his beta, and had done all he could to keep him close but apart. They had kissed once, and later, he'd nearly fucked Kristoff on his desk. He recalled the curve of Kristoff's sweet round ass, his dick pointed toward home, but then he'd seen the picture he still had of Sarai and was about to turn away when they were interrupted by a knock on the door.

That had been the last time either of them had acknowledged their need for each other. Or it had been the last time Jeremiah had allowed himself to see the pain and the brokenness he'd left behind. But they'd had important things to focus on then as well. Alonya had wanted to take over Kristoff's nephew's pack and had been out for blood.

Well, she was dead now, fried to ash by a vindictive Peter bent on saving his mate as well as his uncle. Still, she had damaged Kristoff, and his mate had decided it was better for all if he were no longer there. Kristoff blamed his weakness, his vulnerability. Jeremiah blamed himself.

And now they had Stefan. All Jeremiah wanted was to take Kristoff home to Kentucky, present him as his mate to their pack, and fuck him so hard he wouldn't be able to ever leave him again. He wanted him back at his side.

"Stefan is after something, but instead of coming to me directly, he went to Mrs. Hilliard. Why?"

Jeremiah wiped his mouth and set his napkin down. "I don't know. Fear. Maybe he's afraid of you. Afraid of what you can do to him."

"No, I don't think that's it. Stefan was never one to admit his own vulnerability. He has a reason why he's choosing not to face me. I worry that this is only the first movement in a war we are blind to. I've heard nothing from the man in years, and now word comes that he is looking for me, and his first strike is to visit Mrs. Hilliard." Kristoff leaned back, his neck exposed, the marks Jeremiah made vivid against his pale skin.

Jeremiah's wolf rumbled with satisfaction. "I would agree. He is planning something, and whatever it is, we're not going to like it, but we'll face it together."

"Together?" Kristoff stood then, retrieving his plate and

Jeremiah's.

"Yes, Kristoff. We are one, you and I. Have we not always been, *cara*?" Kristoff was his love, and he needed him to know it. He encircled Kristoff's wrist before he could move away. "Always." He pulled Kristoff closer, and the plates fell to the table, clattering. "I need your mouth on mine."

"Fuck, Jeremiah," Kristoff moaned.

"I would love that more than the rising sun, Kristoff, but you are not ready for that. So I will take this instead."

For Jeremiah, Kristoff's mouth was heaven on earth, and delving within its depths gave him more joy than he had known in years. Kristoff moaned hungrily, and he reveled at the sound. His heart sang at the pleasure of Kristoff's taste, the sweetness of molasses on his tongue too delightful to resist. He pulled Kristoff onto his lap.

This time it was Kristoff who was growling as the kiss deepened. Jeremiah held on tighter, his hand at the back of Kristoff's head as he took all his mate had to offer. Jeremiah's dick was hard in the jeans he'd chosen to imprison it in, ready to provide the path to freedom through the zipper.

"Jeremiah," Kristoff whispered. "Please."

"I know, sweetheart. I know. Me, too." Jeremiah lifted Kristoff and stood. He pressed hungry kisses against Kristoff's neck, nibbling at his skin, so tempted to sink his canines in and leave his claiming mark permanently on his mate. Instead, he took a deep breath, calming the staccato beating of his heart. "Okay. Just needed a taste." He eased away from Kristoff before he took him right there on the table. He picked up the plates while Kristoff sat still, staring at him. He had questions. Jeremiah knew he did. "Let's put these away and get out of here. I'd like to see the reason you love this place so much that you would hide here for almost a year rather than come home."

"I wasn't hiding."

"Selling yourself a bridge, are you?"

Jeremiah laughed, relishing Kristoff's growl of frustration as he walked away.

CHAPTER EIGHT

Kristoff continued to growl. Jeremiah was an asshole. Everyone thought the man walked on water, but he was an arrogant ass. He barked, and his packed jumped. Fucker.

Well, Kristoff wasn't jumping. Okay, he was taking Jeremiah out as he'd asked. But it was only because he wanted to, not because the fucker had demanded to see his city. No, it was not.

And who did Jeremiah think he was? Suddenly appearing to give Kristoff everything he ever wanted only to snatch it away when Kristoff least expected it? Because that was what would happen, wasn't it? Only last night, he'd sucked Kristoff's brains out, and after that kiss . . . Fuck.

He was a goner, wasn't he?

No, he had better control than that. He hadn't risen to the level he had in life to be cowed. Not by himself, not by Stefan, and not by Jeremiah.

So what if just the thought of Jeremiah's naked skin next to his made him harder than granite, and the need to have his hole filled by the man he still loved nearly broke him.

What had Jeremiah said?

We'll face it together. We are one.

Broken Promises. That's all they would be, because just like he'd done years ago, Jeremiah would ignore their bond, and Kristoff would be left shivering in the cold.

He felt the buzzing at his hip and picked up his phone.

Peter. Again.

His nephew had given up trying to reach him by phone

months ago and had begun to rely on text messages. As much as he could, he'd advised him. Peter was the leader of a large coven in Russia and had traveled back home with his human mate. Remi was a good man, a worthy ally who had risked his own life and had accepted his duties as mate to the Korol, king of an ancient race of vampires, the nelapsi. There were many who were not happy to learn they were now to be led by a half-breed—an abomination of vampire and wolf mix—along with his lesser human mate. The moment the two stepped off the plane with their motley entourage of two vampires, two wolves, another human, a fairy, and a sandman—because Aiden was still trying to prove his use to the family who already loved and accepted him—there had been an assassination attempt.

Fully into his power, his nephew had frozen the attackers mid-stride with a lift of his hand and crushed them to a pulp where they stood. Instead of being impressed, this action had only caused more unrest and fear within the coven. He'd advised Peter to maintain his position, though. Sadly, there were those who only respect force, and would hold their people captive in ignorance to keep the blood pure.

Regrettably, Kristoff had not supported the union of Peter and Remi at first, but he'd come to respect Remi. How could he not, seeing the way the man cared so deeply for Peter?

It was time for progress, and Peter would be a part of that move forward. He and his band of misfits.

For the first time in months, Kristoff picked up the phone and called, smiling wickedly when Peter's shock at actually hearing his uncle's voice came across the line.

"Uncle?"

"Hello, nephew."

"It's good to hear your voice."

"Yes. It's been a while. How are you?"

"Tired. It would be easier to kill them all."

"Yes, perhaps. Would you like some help with that?"

Peter's laughter was music in the wind. He'd missed the boy, the echo of his sister's melodious voice reflected in her son's tone. She and her mate had been killed by the same ancient members of the coven Peter was trying to drag into the present. Kristoff had little sympathy for them. Still, he had promised his sister and her husband to be there for their son years ago when they'd realized their child was in danger. Both his sister and her mate had given all they had to protect their young one, running over land and sea, purchasing the home where Kristoff now lived, making a home, a sanctuary.

Now that child was an adult, living on Kristoff's home continent, the burden of his responsibilities weighing him down.

"No, Uncle." Peter laughed derisively. "You were right before when you told me to be fair and consistent, fitting in my judgment when the time comes. Some have challenged me as you said they would, even though they know I wield the full power of the Korol."

"They don't care about that, Peter. The hate they've carried for eons far outweighs common sense and the pride they should have in the strength of their leader. Alexi and Lidiya . . ."

"Should have stayed and fought. I know, but they didn't. And as you've said many times, I can and will be better. Perhaps I just needed to say it out loud, so I could hear it." He sighed. "Thank you."

"You're welcome. It's why I'm here."

"Yes, but why are you there and not at home with Jeremiah? Oh, that's right. Jeremiah is there with you."

"Peter," Kristoff warned.

"I was just asking a question, Uncle. Making an observation. I remember a time when you did the same for me."

"When you wouldn't claim your human? This is not the same."

"What is it exactly? Word is the alpha passed his duties off to Conner and took off to get his beta back home."

Was that how things appeared to those in Kentucky? Kristoff wasn't sure how he felt about that. On the one hand, Jeremiah had dropped everything to rush to his side. The thought of that made him see possibilities he only wanted to ignore, have hope when he'd finally accepted there was none.

On the other hand, did Jeremiah's leaving give the wrong impression? That he was vulnerable? Jeremiah had been challenged before, but by putting his son in his place, was he actually making a statement? Showing them a path the future could take? Jeremiah was always thinking, always planning. Kristoff could not be the sole reason for his presence here.

"Yes, he's here."

"And so?"

"And so nothing, nephew. He is here simply as a friend."

"A friend who's finally pulled his head out of his ass and might just be ready to replace said head with your cock."

"Peter!"

"Uncle Kristoff! Stop acting like you two haven't been sniffing around each other for years. He's yours if you want him."

"You know nothing."

"I know enough. What I don't know, his sons will tell me. They're ready for their father to move on, to get out of their lives, and have one of his own. Most importantly, a whole alpha is a solid alpha."

"As you are."

Peter laughed. "Yes, if you must throw a lesson in. In fact, my mate is . . . Oh, Goddess . . ." The dirty moan Peter let out was a sign that this conversation had come to an end. "Yes. Right there. Uncle . . ."

"You have to go. I know. Tell your *mate* hello for me." With a laugh, Kristoff ended the call. He had been prepared to ask how Remi was faring, but it appeared he didn't have to.

Kristoff looked at the phone in his hand and smiled. Talking to Peter warmed him inside. He would do it more often. It was about time to stop hiding, enjoy his family, and be present. He'd made a promise not only to his sister but to himself. Yes, he'd failed him once, but no more. He would keep his focus and his promise.

In the other room waited a man who was once his alpha, who still was if Kristoff allowed himself to be honest about it. Jeremiah said he wanted to see his home, see what he loved about the city so much. Kristoff could show him, try to share the peace he gained from being so near the ocean he could walk to it. Some nights he did, when he was too restless to sleep.

They would start with the basket weavers, see the market where the tourists flocked, and maybe end the night with a visit to Folly Beach where the locals hung out.

Later, Kristoff drove his sports sedan along Meeting Street, searching for a place to park. He'd thought about riding his bike, but having Jeremiah hang on to him while they traversed the roads would have driven him mad. The feel of Jeremiah's cock against his ass was not something he could handle with aplomb at the moment. So, the car it was. It was safer that way, at least for his libido. His mind couldn't stop thinking about yesterday on the floor at Jeremiah's mercy and even earlier with the kiss. He desired Jeremiah just as much if not more than his wolf did. But to go down that road again?

No, he wouldn't think about that. They would visit the Historic Charleston City Market so Jeremiah could see the basket weavers. Kristoff had earned their trust years ago, and they would actually allow him to practice there. In his heart of hearts, he was an artist, and he appreciated art in all its forms. Seeing the women and men weave sweetgrass baskets and then being given the opportunity to learn the skill was thera-peutic for him.

More importantly, it was history. A craft passed down from generation to generation. The only thing his father had ever passed to him was the knowledge of weaponry and how many different ways there were to take a life. His love of painting had been treated as a pastime. He was a wolf trained to perform his duty, to take care of his alpha as the wolves of his family before him.

But he was also a man.

A man who wanted to crawl onto the lap of the man next to him and tell him exactly where to put that long hard cock of his.

He parked.

CHAPTER NINE

Jeremiah noted Kristoff's quiet as he exited the car, the cool veneer he wore as enticing to him as a scent he needed to chase. He'd never been this hungry before, or perhaps he had. He'd simply ignored his own needs in favor of holding onto memories. Sarai would have encouraged him to love again, but he'd chosen to remain frozen inside, savoring the bits of warmth he was able to gather from Kristoff's light.

Now that he was allowing himself to live again, to see what he could possibly have with Kristoff, he was not merely hungry, he was ravenous. What he didn't want to do was push Kristoff too hard, cause him to retreat, plan, then disappear. The wolf could do it, too. He had been known to vanish without a trace. It went against Jeremiah's nature to allow that to happen, especially now that his wolf was ready to claim his mate. Instead of wherever they now stood, Jeremiah wanted to be buried balls deep inside the heat of his mate's opening, his claws thrust into Kristoff's flanks, his mouth drinking Kristoff's blood as he struck.

The two walked together, maneuvering through the crowds. Jeremiah reached with his mind, his essence traveling along with Kristoff's energy, testing, prodding for a response.

"You know I can feel you, alpha. Pull back or prepare to fight," Kristoff growled.

"You think that a threat, Kristoff, *mo grá*. The thought of my flesh against yours in battle only makes my dick hard enough to chisel rock." He brushed against Kristoff, savoring the closeness of their bodies, and smiling when the crowd helped to conceal his efforts.

Kristoff shook his head, and Jeremiah recognized the lines of humor both on his sharp face and sparking through his essence. He licked at Kristoff's energy, then savored the barely concealed shiver.

"Your love, hm? You are worse than a pup, alpha." Mockery tinged Kristoff's tone. "Let's go. If we're quick, we can catch Mary and her son, Phillipe. They're the only ones who have allowed me close enough to practice beside them."

"You still haven't told me what we've come here to see, beta."

"Not your beta anymore, Jeremiah," Kristoff argued.

"Perhaps that is true, Kristoff, since you are my mate."

Kristoff's long strides pressed forward in an obvious attempt to leave Jeremiah behind.

Jeremiah slowed down to appreciate the view of Kristoff's plump ass, eager to take a bite later. He took a moment to study the humans around him. He scented the air, separating the aromas, distinguishing the hint of sugared pralines—a treat Kristoff had shared with him once before—from the incense and other enticements that wafted past his nose. Pleased there were not any recognizable scents of danger, he followed behind Kristoff at a distance, only coming up short when he found his mate searching, a feeling of dread permeating the air about him.

Jeremiah neared him, listening.

"Gone."

"What do you mean, gone?" Kristoff questioned.

Kristoff was speaking to a man scented with frustration. The accent the man spoke in was lyrical, reminding Jeremiah of tropical islands and drums. His brown eyes were watchful as he sat on a padded towel, basket in hand weaving.

"I mean that last night Mary and Phillipe say don' go to the market. There be dark ones creeping about, moonwalkers.

She say, *You tell da boy, Kristoff, there's things hunting him that no one wants to see.* She and her boy pack up and went to her sistah's house." The man stopped weaving and reached underneath his shirt.

Jeremiah noticed the minute shift in Kristoff's stance, the ready alertness. Instead of a weapon, a shiny glint of metal fell into the man's dark hand.

"I ain't worried 'bout no moonwalkers," he said. "Got me a cross made of silver and de prayers of the Lord. Got me bills to pay and another mouth to feed. Now, you? You carry on from here. The devil's on your shoulder, looking for souls to steal. You ain't wanted no mo'."

Jeremiah touched Kristoff's arm, not surprised to feel the rigidness of his muscles.

"Kristoff."

"Stefan. It has to be," Kristoff growled.

"Where does Mary's sister live?" Jeremiah asked.

"Now, moonwalker, I ain't goin' tell you that. We all tell her, tell Mary to leave that moonwalker alone, but she think you so pretty with your silver hair and them ice blue eyes of yours. We tell her you no good, only goin' bring danger 'round here. Now, she up and run. I don't know what scared her, but I ain't Mary. You go on." The basket weaver ignored them both and went back to work. With nothing left to say, they drifted away beyond the weaver's hearing.

"We'll get it sorted, Kristoff. I promise." *Moonwalkers?* "Stefan is human, isn't he?" Jeremiah had to wonder. First a wolf that shifted before a human, and now moonwalkers.

"Yes, nothing more. I would have known it."

Would he? Maybe with all of Kristoff's observational skills and military astuteness, he'd had a lapse. No one was perfect. Not even Kristoff.

"I understand how perceptive you are, and how you miss nothing, but perhaps just this once—"

"No. What wolf would have allowed himself to be placed in a cell surrounded by humans? Would he not have escaped years ago? He's human."

"If so, then why is he suddenly surrounded by *moonwalkers*, as we've just heard?" He used the term, trying it on his lips. It was the first time he'd ever heard their people called that. He rather liked it.

"You like the name, don't you?"

"It's a little interesting, yes." He snorted. "What do you want to do now, since we won't be able to basketweave? And killing the messenger there won't help, so stop threatening him."

"I haven't said a word to the human."

"My beautiful Kristoff, you never need words to convey what you feel, especially when it concerns me."

Kristoff's glacial blue eyes stared at him, peering beneath his surface. There was nothing to discover. He was here for Kristoff, ready to fight for him, kill for him, and hopefully gain his trust again.

Kristoff shook his head. "I'm frustrated. I don't know what Stefan wants, why he is circling me rather than meeting me head-on. What is his endgame? Perhaps I should go to him."

"Perhaps *we* should go to him."

Kristoff turned to lean against an ancient brick wall, and Jeremiah was glad to be out of the oscillating path of the shoppers as they sought treasure among the many vendors present.

Kristoff crossed his arms, his biceps like boulders and his shoulders wide and squeezable. He looked skyward. "Jeremiah, I don't want you there when I face Stefan."

Jeremiah sighed. "That will be a problem, then, as I intend to be there. You will not fight him alone." He moved into his mate's space, bending to inhale his scent, the spiciness of Kristoff's skin. He longed to taste and to touch.

"Not here, Jeremiah. There are too many eyes."

"Then they will see me kiss my mate. All the better for them to see what love looks like."

"This isn't love. I don't know what this is, or when your own eyes will clear. I won't be left behind when you decide I'm not worthy when I already know this."

"And why are you not worthy, Kristoff? Why can't I love you?"

Kristoff sighed, but his body opened to let Jeremiah in.

His wolf stretched forward in pleasure, delighted to have his mate near again. He aligned their bodies, notched his head into the crook of Kristoff's shoulder and neck, taking a deep breath. Wrapping his arms around Kristoff, he held him close.

"Your scent is driving me mad, *mo grá*." Jeremiah groaned from his restraint. He traced his lips along Kristoff's neck, breathing in his scent and laughing when he moaned.

"Since when did I become *your love*, Jeremiah? I don't understand this, no matter how much I've wanted it. I don't know why you've changed. Whatever has you here insisting you love me, accept me — I can't trust it. I can't trust you."

The words cut deep, and Jeremiah lifted him. "You've never had a reason to question me before, Kristoff," he growled.

"At my back, as we fought together, yes. With my heart? No. It is too much to ask, especially now." Kristoff pressed his hands against Jeremiah's chest, moving him back. "And right now, this isn't what I need. It isn't helping me. I lost focus once, and my nephew nearly lost his mate. I could have lost Peter and . . . and you. Who knows how far Alonya would have gone?"

"She's dead, Kristoff. I'm here."

"Yes, you are, Jeremiah, but for how long? That's a risk I don't wish to take."

The effect of Jeremiah's previous rejection of Kristoff must have been significant if he was revealing his thoughts, his inner turmoil. His mate wasn't that type of man, that type of wolf. Kristoff typically kept his secrets, his vulnerabilities, close to his chest.

Jeremiah sighed. "I'm not a risk to you, Kristoff."

Kristoff nodded but turned away. "While we can't participate in the weaving, we can at least observe."

Jeremiah's wolf didn't care for the abrupt change in topics, but he listened as Kristoff explained the artistry of basket weaving, smiling at his enthusiasm. This was a side of Kristoff the pack didn't know, maybe not even his nephew. The silent and powerful Kristoff enjoyed art in all its forms. Often when Kristoff traveled to Paris, Israel, or even Ireland, he took the time to visit places where the great artists of days gone past had trained. It wasn't common knowledge to most, but in his heart, the wolf Jeremiah wanted as his own was an artist. The evidence showed in the arresting painting hanging in his dining room, and now as he revealed tidbits he had learned and techniques he shared with Jeremiah.

Hours later, after they'd visited the different vendors, picking up an item here or there, the two of them were hungry. The sadness that had weighed his mate down no longer plagued his expression, and his cheeks reddened with the excitement of bargaining for a few treasures.

"You enjoyed yourself there, it seems," Jeremiah surmised.

Kristoff popped the trunk and carefully placed the items inside.

How many baskets, carved animals, leather binders, and handmade incense holders does a wolf need? Apparently, many.

"Always. The haggling is expected. It was fun." Kristoff's careless laughter was a thing to behold, the way it danced in the air — its essence nearly shimmering with joy.

Jeremiah loved watching Kristoff. Seeing the man he adored unguarded for a moment was a prayer answered.

Kristoff rounded the car and got inside. Jeremiah quickly followed, as eager as the youth he was sometimes accused of being.

"I'm usually by myself, so there's no one to celebrate the spoils with, but with you . . ." Kristoff trailed off and shook his head, apparently realizing what he'd said. He sighed and started the car.

"It was fun, and I enjoyed seeing you in your element, whittling down prices with nary a harsh word between you and your victims. I'd like more of that, Kristoff."

Kristoff nodded and pulled into traffic. "I think we should eat, then perhaps drive down to the beach."

"I would like that. It's been a while since I've had a walk on the shore, placed my feet on the sand." Jeremiah paused. "A run as wolves would be nice."

It would also free Kristoff's wolf from the binds his mate held on it. Its nature would be there, submissive to its alpha, unable to resist its mate. Kristoff was formidable in both forms, but he was vulnerable to their bond when he shed his human form.

The icy glare Kristoff sent his way indicated he knew very well the path his alpha was thinking.

"It may well be, but I think it best to avoid that for now. People and daylight. Human forms for now, and food before heading home."

Jeremiah smiled. "Ah, of course. Another time."

Kristoff sped out of the parking lot, but Jeremiah could tell he wasn't the only one thinking of other times to be had. Kristoff's firm grasp on the wheel, the overwhelming scent of his need, and his mate's focus on the road were signs enough for him.

Instead of letting it go, Jeremiah leaned over into Kristoff's heat and gripped the cock tightly hidden inside his jeans. "I think it will be worth the wait."

Kristoff gasped. "Fuck you, Jeremiah." He moaned as Jeremiah unzipped his pants, then whimpered as Jeremiah bent low to inhale his mate's scent.

"Can't wait, *mo grá*." He chuckled. "For now, another taste."

Jeremiah had to admire Kristoff's control as he took his length down his throat.

CHAPTER TEN

They were going to die, but Kristoff would know no pain, only joy as his seed filled the hollows of Jeremiah's cheeks. In moments, he and the man he loved would fly off the bridge and sink to the bottom of the ocean where they would become a meal to feed the scavengers that waited there.

How he kept the car pointed in the direction of Folly Beach, he had no idea, because his brains were currently being sucked out through his dick. The wetness and the suction were heaven, and the press of Jeremiah's tongue against his glands only made him hunger for more.

"Please, Jeremiah," he begged. He didn't know whether he was pleading for the man to stop or to open his throat wider so he could fuck his way in, fill him with his cum and his essence.

Submit. Submit.

The words repeated like a broken record in his mind, his wolf urging him to accept, to submit, and to please. Kristoff couldn't. No matter how incredible the feeling was to have Jeremiah's lips wrapped around his dick, his breath tickling his balls, he fought the desire and his own need.

He trembled, but his hands remained locked on the wheel as he thrust into Jeremiah's heat.

"Jeremiah."

Jeremiah hummed in response, sliding his mouth slowly off his dick. "Yes, Kristoff."

"You can't do this."

"Can't I?"

"Oh, Goddess."

Kristoff moaned as Jeremiah sucked him in again, his head rising and falling, the blue-black of his hair a blur as he took Kristoff out of orbit, drinking his cum and growling in pleasure. Kristoff's breath rushed in and out, his heart drumming a solo that echoed in his ears. The thumping in his chest finally slowed when they pulled into the parking lot at the beach. "You. I hate you," he grumbled.

Jeremiah settled back with a smile on his face. "No, my love, you don't. Far from it. You've only to accept it, so we can go home."

Kristoff knew the home Jeremiah meant wasn't in Charleston. Jeremiah wanted to take him back to the pack, to continue living a life he thought he'd left behind.

Could he? Could he start over again? Be the person he was before he adopted Charleston as his sanctuary?

Kristoff put his limp cock back inside his pants, waiting until he was out of the car to fully put himself together again.

Go home.

This was home for him now. He liked his house, his neighbors, a place to return to that gave him peace. Yes, it was quiet. There weren't hundreds of people he helped govern along with an alpha who was currently trying to dismantle his sanity. He missed his nephew and their growing family, meeting the coven he was dragging into the 21st century. But Kristoff was no longer worried about failing those he loved. Hiding, maybe, but he chose to call it protecting himself.

Okay, he was hiding.

He thought back to Mrs. Hilliard and Mary, two people he'd grown to care for, and how neither was accessible to him any longer. Had he made a mistake somewhere? Was staying here as long as he had and developing relationships the best decision? It seemed that no matter where he went, there were people to love even when he failed to realize that love was indeed what he felt.

There were so many questions, and for once, Kristoff didn't feel like he had the answers.

Setting himself fully to rights, he pocketed his keys. He turned to Jeremiah, who looked at him with such heat Kristoff felt the need to step back before the flames completely knocked him off his feet. The alpha called to him regardless of his wolf, the man stalked him around the car, advancing on him, and the waves of pheromones assailing him took his breath away. Jeremiah became the very air he needed to breathe.

Kristoff struck out over the sand as fast as his feet would carry him, his shoes beating against the hot sand. If he was near people, Jeremiah would have to veer off course, pretend to be human rather than the beast Kristoff knew he was barely restraining.

When Kristoff made it to an area where people stood, some coming from the ocean and others preparing to enter, he took a deep breath. Safe. Then he felt arms around him, lips at his neck, and he moaned, his entire body, his soul submitting to the master of his heart.

"Why do you run, Kristoff? My beautiful, resilient, dangerous wolf?"

"Because I fear for my heart when you are near, Jeremiah. I fear that your presence will render me in two."

Sharp points pierced his skin, sliding into his neck, staking claim as Jeremiah's tongue licked roughly. Kristoff glanced around the periphery, but no one seemed to notice his predicament or even care.

"Years ago, I was a fool not to embrace you, to be grateful that the Goddess chose you for me. I won't make that mistake again. I need you to know this," Jeremiah murmured.

Kristoff pulled against Jeremiah but failed to force the man to let him go. But did he truly want to, or did he crave Jeremiah's hold, his power, the way his strength made him feel safe?

Surrendering, Kristoff leaned back against his alpha and let his head fall against his shoulder.

"There you are. Rest. I have you, just as I will tonight. Tonight, my love, my wolf, I will claim you."

Kristoff shivered. "Jeremiah."

"Shh. For now, let's walk. Later, I'll fill your hole with my seed and drink from that pretty long neck of yours. And, if you want to run, that's okay. I'm here to catch you."

A frisbee landed against Kristoff's shoe, and he looked up to see a blond-haired little waif waiting hopefully. The urchin appeared a sweet creature, his eyes bright and shiny, new and unburdened. Kristoff was wistful for a moment. To be that carefree, the only urgent concern the desire to play a game of frisbee. Had Kristoff ever had the chance to be that little one? No.

From the moment he could carry a weapon with a grip small enough for his little hands at five years old, he was taught to shoot. He'd also learned three different forms of martial arts and half a dozen ways to kill a man. Even at such a young age, he could hold his own against three teenagers twice his size.

He'd never been anything like this little boy.

Jeremiah released him, and Kristoff picked up the frisbee to toss it back to the child, who ran after it on legs as fast as a gazelle. He watched carefully that no harm came to the little boy until he made it to his family, who were oblivious to the fact they'd temporarily lost their treasure.

An arm wrapped around him, and he and Jeremiah left the family behind.

"What do you want to do?" Jeremiah asked after a moment.

At his side for many years, Kristoff knew the alpha's thoughts. They were his own many times. The two of them had always complimented each other. It was what made them such a formidable team, both in battle and at the head of the Iroquois Pack. It didn't mean they always agreed. There were times when Kristoff truly felt Jeremiah was out of his mind. Like when he thought it was a good idea to open the pack grounds to humans to tour the facility and encourage business partnerships.

Kristoff believed stoutly in tradition and in keeping the pack safe, insular. Jeremiah felt the pack needed to grow, and for that to happen, they needed to shed the fears of vulnerability. He had submitted to Kristoff's request for increased security and restricted areas on the grounds, though. Jeremiah had also put Kristoff in charge of delegating the roles that necessary pack members would play to ensure safety for all, particularly the young.

In the end, the outcome had been growth, and Jeremiah's pack had gained a crucial foothold in the community surrounding them. Their furniture was sought after, their security was hired, and their youth were able to attend surrounding universities, having adjusted well through the introduction to the human schools. The young knew how to act human, what the expectations were, and where the safe places for their kind were. The pack had branched out, and some had even been able to live in the human world. There were drawbacks, of course, but that was to be expected.

Sometimes a human mate was discovered, and a wolf denied his mate was a terrible thing. It was a problem that had to be handled, and unfortunately, there were times when a loved one was left weeping on both sides. The inability to cross the divide was sometimes too difficult, leaving the mates without their other half. The lack of fulfillment was detrimental to their mental state. If they weren't strong enough or didn't have a support system, sometimes the desire to end such an empty life was greater. It was a reality no one wished to deal with, but it had to be done.

A wolf denied his mate was a concept Kristoff could relate to. How many years had he lived denied by Jeremiah? Now here they stood in reversed roles. This time it was he who wished to deny his mate and Jeremiah who refused to be denied.

"Stephan is playing a game of cat and mouse, visiting people I know, staying on the periphery. He wants me to know he can get to me, that it's only a matter of time."

"We could go home, back to Louisville."

"I don't think I'm ready for that, that I'll ever be ready, Jeremiah. I've moved forward. To return there would be a mistake."

Jeremiah put a hand on Kristoff's shoulder and turned him to face him. Those warm eyes, bottomless and all-seeing, looked deep within. "I made mistakes, ones that I would apologize for daily if you'd only allow me by your side again."

Kristoff backed away, out of Jeremiah's reach.

Jeremiah would not be thwarted and stepped forward, into Kristoff's space. "I want to fix this, fix us."

"I don't think we can. I don't trust you. I don't trust myself."

Jeremiah nodded, but there was a fire in his gorgeous eyes. "We *can* fix this, Kristoff. And you know better. You can trust me, and you can trust yourself. You're living a lie if you try to believe otherwise." Jeremiah captured his lips, his tongue diving deep. He broke the kiss briefly to add, "To you, to me, and to our wolves. Fortunately for us, your wolf has better sense than its human."

Kristoff moaned hungrily as his wolf yearned for its mate. Jeremiah shoved him hard against the car. His legs readily parted wide to allow his alpha closer.

"I could fuck you right here, right now, Kristoff. And you'd let me. You want to believe that you can stand against me, that you can stop me, but I know how much you need me, how your soul craves its partner. You are desperate to have me inside you, filling your sweet body, mastering you as I should."

Jeremiah's teeth were against Kristoff's neck, dancing over his earlier marks.

"But I need you, too," he whispered. "Just as much as you need me, if not more. I need to be a part of you completely. I need to make you mine, to forge my iron within you. I need to master you, to own you, body and soul. I need you to submit to me, to allow me to protect you. I need us to be one. And I'm not above begging for the chance, Kristoff. Please let me in."

Kristoff's head fell back against the car's roof as Jeremiah's scent assailed him, overwhelmed him. "Jeremiah."

"I won't fail you, Kristoff. Let me have you fully. Trust in me, in yourself. Listen to your wolf. I've heard its cry as it seeks its alpha."

Jeremiah pressed his length against Kristoff, the hardness of his body what Kristoff craved. No matter how many miles he ran, how many countries he traveled, or how many missions he completed, the need to be beneath his alpha chased him. And here Jeremiah was asking for the very thing Kristoff needed, what he'd been running from when he thought he would never have it.

"Please, Kristoff," Jeremiah begged as he kissed him, his voice brushing over Kristoff's soul. His lips were urgent, and the sharp points of his teeth were destroying Kristoff. "Let me have you, all of you."

Kristoff tested Jeremiah's hold, sighing with pleasure when Jeremiah's strength refused to give. Jeremiah growled a warning, and Kristoff moaned. He was secure. He was safe.

"I have you, my wolf. Your alpha, your protector, and your keeper. Your mate, Kristoff. Tonight, I'm taking you, and then we'll figure this out together. Get your ass in the car and take us back to your home."

CHAPTER ELEVEN

Kristoff was trying to drive, his dick cupped possessively in Jeremiah's palm as he raced back to his home. He hadn't said yes to Jeremiah, but they both knew what his answer would be. What it had always been.

Kristoff had been lying to himself, telling himself and his wolf they denied Jeremiah when it had only been a matter of time. Had Jeremiah not arrived to warn him of Stefan, how much longer would it have been before he made the decision to chase his demons and seek out the keeper of his heart?

They rode together in silence, but the throbbing of their hearts was a drum section. Kristoff could nearly hear Jeremiah's beat blocking out his own. The eagerness to get home, to get under his mate, was like an overwhelming tide rushing onto the shore.

"Drive faster," Jeremiah said.

"Trying not to get a ticket, alpha," Kristoff growled. He was just as ready. The blood in his hard dick pulsed urgently as he thought of all the things he wanted Jeremiah to do to him and the things he wanted to do to Jeremiah.

The sun was going down, the orange glow of the horizon drifting away, leaving the moon's sweet kiss. How fitting that the two of them would unite on a night where the moon was full. How apt. Perhaps it was the Goddess blessing them, pleased with them both as they finally accepted each other. Their wolves would finally be allowed to join, to love, to claim, and to be mated forever.

"We could pull to the side of the road, Kristoff, find an out of the way place—"

"No. I want . . . I need . . ." Kristoff's face grew warm as he reached for the words. "I want our first time, the moment we claim one another to be in my home, in my bed. After that, who knows? But tonight? Our first night? I need to show you've what I've prayed to have for so long."

Jeremiah's intake of breath in response was clear. Yeah, Kristoff felt the same way. After so much time, so many years, they would take the next step.

The sun had fully set by the time they arrived at the end of Kristoff's street, the scent of flames reaching them first. It was easy for two wolves to detect, and the whir of firetrucks that sped by only confirmed there was a home on fire.

"Shit." Kristoff drove faster, testing the car's boasted acceleration to its limit.

"The good thing is Mrs. Hilliard is gone."

Yes, for that, Kristoff was grateful. Now, he just needed to follow the sirens and see what the hell was going on.

As he pulled up near what used to be his home, and once the beloved home of his sister and her young family, Kristoff's heart shattered in his chest. The blood rushed between his ears, and his wolf threatened to erupt from within.

"No." He shoved himself from the car, his feet on the ground, ready to run, to do something, to save his home, the last of what he had left of his sister . . . his sanctuary.

"Stop, Kristoff. My beta, my love. Stop. There's nothing you can do."

Arms wrapped around him, pulling him tight against a hard chest. The flames danced out of the windows, and the smoke billowed. It was a living breathing thing, mangling and destroying as it coursed through the house's structure.

"Nothing. I have nothing."

"No, Kristoff. No, my darling. You have me."

Kristoff fought back the tears, refusing to acknowledge the

wetness at the corner of his eyes. He would not be weak, would not be destroyed. Instead, Kristoff would be angry. Volatile. There was no fucking way this had just happened. Kristoff knew who did this. He didn't know why. Why would Stefan take things this far? Kristoff could have killed him, but he'd let him live.

And this is how he was repaid.

Kristoff would correct the mistake he'd made so long ago. This time, he'd kill the fucker.

Because now he'd left Kristoff with only one place to go.

Home.

Kristoff's skin began to itch the moment he saw the white fences. The moment, the very second they'd finished with the police, the fire chief, and insurance, Jeremiah did not hesitate to completely take over Kristoff's life. He had bundled him and the few possessions he had, then got them both in his car on the way back to Louisville, Kentucky.

So, fences. White fences.

White fences bordering grassy land speckled with horses. Kristoff was on his way to the compound. To a place he'd left behind months ago after he'd decided he couldn't trust himself not to endanger the family he'd grown to love, the people he'd come to care for.

How was returning with the possibility of Stefan causing mayhem any better?

"He could come here," Kristoff said for probably the fifth time since they'd started this journey.

"He's probably already here," Jeremiah agreed.

"Then why?"

"Because if you're going to fight him, it needs to be on your territory. He needs to know you're not alone. I think that's why he was doing this, to take everything from you. He wants you vulnerable. This distance could give us a chance to learn just why that is, but it will definitely bring you added protection."

"I can do this—"

"By yourself. I know. But, my wolf, you don't have to. You have a family here, one that loves you, one that knows you." Jeremiah placed his hand on Kristoff's thigh as he veered around a car that was apparently driving too slow for him.

Jeremiah was known for his lead foot. He was a patient alpha who governed his people passionately and with love. But Jeremiah was a menace on the road, and Kristoff had nearly asked him several times if he could take over. It would be futile, so he focused on Jeremiah's words rather than the way other cars quickly became dots in his passenger mirror.

"You have me, and don't forget we have some unfinished business." Jeremiah's fingers drifted along Kristoff's thigh, making him shiver.

There went another car, but Kristoff didn't give a fuck. He was too focused on the way the tips of Jeremiah's fingers kneaded the muscles in his thighs. His dick swelled in his pants, and he almost reached toward his zipper with the intent to give it the free reign it craved.

When his phone rang, it was an unwelcome surprise.

"Uncle Kristoff."

It was Samuel, one of Connor's brood. Jeremiah's oldest son and his mate, a sprite, had, at last count, eight children, with Samuel being number five. He was a dangerous creature with an insatiable passion for life in all its forms, flighty as a butterfly. It would take a person wielding a far-reaching net to capture him.

"Yes, boy."

"I'm sure Grandfather is driving, so I figured I'd call you. You're coming home, right?"

Home. Kristoff hadn't wanted to, but how could he fight

the need to be with Jeremiah? He had to be honest with himself.

"Yes. Why?" He was almost afraid of the answer. With Samuel, it could be anything.

"Well, my dad is busy with pack business, and my mom has to take care of the youngest ones, so no one really noticed at first, but now, since they're all home this weekend, they have, and I already told him he could stay. So, he's in my room, in my bed actually. And he's so good. So tasty. I just wanted a little more of him. But Dad says I broke pack law and wants to kill him. Mom says that I really fucked up. I said, *Let's talk to Grandfather*, but then someone said you'd be here, and you know, maybe, you could talk to them."

"Breathe, Samuel. What did you do?" Kristoff already felt the beginnings of a headache, a Samuel sized one.

"Well, I played at a club last night. Dad said I could as long as I was good."

Good to Samuel was relative. It could mean he didn't fly through the room as he sprouted wings from his back. Or that he didn't spin people around an arena like a tornado shocking the audience as he called the wind to his fingertips. Both had happened before and had been PR nightmares. One never knew exactly what the half-wolf, half-sprite was up to, especially since his favorite human, Darren, was finishing up grad school.

"How good?" Kristoff couldn't believe he was asking this.

"Oh, so good, Uncle Kristoff. I only used a little magic, so there were no orgies. Nothing like that one time. But I had a fan that followed me, and he smelled tantalizing. His essence was divine, and Darren is away at school, and I was hungry, so I decided to keep him."

Shit.

"Is that Samuel I hear?" Jeremiah sighed tiredly.

"Yes, it's your idiot grandson."

"Ah, the sweet bane of my existence. What has the brat

done now?"

"It sounds like he's kept a human locked away in his room to feed on his essence."

Jeremiah's groan warmed Kristoff's heart. His alpha needed him, needed his mate as his balance. Kristoff had served his alpha, and he gave him peace. With the complications that came with one son married to a sprite and the other to a sandman, there were bound to be surprises. Kristoff had helped Jeremiah handle the stress.

"When I get home, young one, you and I will talk about rules again, especially when you know your parents are distracted. Stop fucking her." Kristoff heard the sounds of sex in the background and may have been a little envious.

"Him," Samuel corrected.

"Of course. Him. Stop fucking him and devouring his essence. Humans are not snacks, yes?"

The pregnant pause was enough to make Kristoff grind his teeth. "Samuel?"

"Yes, uncle."

"Where is the human?" Kristoff didn't like the moan he heard.

"Licking my balls like a good boy."

He'd asked. He had known better, but he'd asked. "I won't be a fool and ask you to tell him to stop. When he's done servicing your greedy dick, I want him cleaned up and put in a separate room. I'll speak to your mother about a separation spell, and you will stay away from him."

"But Dad —"

"Your father is frustrated as he should be, you little shit. You have been given more freedom than many. Finish with him, clean him up, and we'll get him on his way. Hopefully, he doesn't have family members looking for him."

"Will you . . ." Samuel's nervousness radiated over the phone.

"Talk to your father. Yes. When I return."

"Oh, yes. That's good. Here. Pour it on and slick it up. Let me see you. So good. Now. Turn around. Your ass is so pretty and round."

Apparently, Kristoff had been forgotten.

"Samuel," Kristoff growled. The minx was so scattered sometimes.

"Oh, sorry. I'm going to fuck him again. I'm so glad you're coming home. We miss you. Spread yourself wider. Right there."

Kristoff winced when the pained shout came across the phone, followed by pleas for more. Shaking his head, he ended the call.

"It would appear things are as normal with my grandson."

"Yes, they are."

"You'll take care of this, yes?"

"Don't I always?"

"Not for some time now."

There was a wealth of emotion in those words, and the broken sound of pain touched Kristoff in a way nothing else could. His alpha, his mate, had needed him, and he hadn't been there to ease the frustrations of handling pack and family. He had to wonder what else was amiss.

"No, but I'm back."

"For how long, Kristoff? What will it take for you to realize this is your true home, that I'm your true home? I made a mistake letting you go, letting you leave believing you failed us somehow."

"I did. I lost sight of what was important, and not only did I nearly die in my error, but much more could have been lost."

"Could have. You're missing the most important details here. Nothing has been lost other than the natural rhythm of my home and the compound. And none of those are the same without you to help me. You are my heart, and you have been so for years. I was simply too blind and selfish in my grief to see it."

Kristoff said nothing, only focused more deeply on the passing white fences. He felt more than heard Jeremiah's deep sigh.

"Do you remember when we first met?"

How could Kristoff not remember? He'd arrived at the Iroquois Pack lands, the compound, as it was called, abandoned and broken. He'd been sent by his former alpha to Jeremiah Tolliver, a young alpha in need of a beta. Kristoff hadn't arrived alone. He'd had Peter with him, his ankle-biter nephew, who was just as broken and lost as his uncle. They'd lost Peter's mother and father, Kristoff's sister and brother-in-law, only weeks before, and Kristoff hadn't known what to do. He couldn't leave Peter by himself. He trusted no one, had lived a life alone for years trusting no one, and it had cost him.

He'd had no one to depend on, no one other than himself and an alpha who had sent him to a new pack.

When he'd arrived on the compound's doorstep, he felt the earth move. There was life there for him, someone there for him. He was needed. It had been overwhelming and earth-shattering.

Then, with young Peter in his arms, he'd met the alpha of the Iriquois pack, and immediately his wolf struggled within to submit to its mate. He'd known the moment Jeremiah laid eyes on him that the alpha knew, that he'd recognized the calling of wolf to wolf, but he'd only shaken his head sadly.

Jeremiah had opened his arms and welcomed Peter as the boy all but jumped into the alpha's arms.

"Yes. I remember."

"I do, too, Kristoff. I remembered the way you smelled, like honey and the forest. I wanted you, needed you then, but Sarai's death was too fresh, too soon, and I could not love another no matter what my wolf screamed. I remember the way

83

you looked at me when Peter allowed me to hold him, like every burden you carried, you would no longer have to suffer alone. Right then, I had my partner, the man who would stand by my side for eternity. And I denied him."

He had. There had been times, moments when the wall of Jeremiah's grief lowered enough for a gentle touch or even the graze of lips. But Kristoff had been pushed away, again and again. He'd still remained hopeful that Jeremiah would let him in one day, would share more than just duty. He'd hoped Jeremiah would share his life.

It had taken Kristoff nearly losing his life to realize that he'd lost his focus and had broken his promise to his sister to keep his nephew safe. That included Peter's mate, who had been kidnapped and tortured. That included Peter's mind and the blood on his hands when he'd had to take Alonya's life. Kristoff's duty was to his family and not solely to the man who would never love him as his mate.

When Peter had Remi back, and he was healed enough, Kristoff had left the pack, thinking he would never return.

Fucking Stefan.

"I made you a promise that day with Peter in my arms. I promised you that you had a home, a promise I broke when I failed to make sure you understood how much you mean to me. But that won't happen again. I won't lose you again. I'm not perfect, Kristoff."

"No one asked you to be perfect, Jeremiah." His eyes burned.

"No, you only asked me to love you. No, before you say it, you never articulated the words. But you didn't have to. I felt them. I knew they were there. I knew you were waiting for me to get my head out of my ass. I'm not too late, Kristoff. I refuse to be too late. You're mine. Now and forever. I won't break another promise to you."

The sun flashed off the bangles Jeremiah wore, but Kristoff

forced himself to keep his gaze on the view outside rather than the man beside him. His heart was so full it felt like it was pressing against his lungs, taking away his ability to breathe.

Can it be so easy?

Could Kristoff finally have the man he loved?

What Jeremiah offered was all Kristoff had ever asked for and had been too afraid to take.

They were quiet for most of the drive back. Jeremiah gave Kristoff time to think, as if he knew that's what he needed.

And he was right.

When they pulled into the compound hours later, something within Kristoff shifted. He looked around at the trees he'd missed, the land he'd walked for years, and the people he'd grown to love and respect. Many waved at him as they drove by, while some nodded as if chastising him for being gone so long. He waved back before he even realized what he was doing.

He'd been fooling himself thinking the house in Charleston was his home. Being on the Iroquois Pack grounds was home for him. This is where he'd found his purpose, where he'd met his mate, and where he'd fallen in love. How could he leave again?

Before he even fully stepped from the vehicle, he was dragged away from Jeremiah, accosted with questions and requests. It would seem there was a party to be held for the first graduates of the human school. The young wolves wanted the humans they'd attended school with to see them on their own territory, to celebrate with them. He'd known this would happen, the need to prove themselves to others. Had he been there, he would have reminded them of how unnecessary it was. Those of true worth could never be ignored. You couldn't eclipse greatness. It was more important to help others shine rather than attempt to be the sun.

He shook his head tiredly as he was dragged to his office, nervous parents in his wake and protesting youth beseeching him to understand. Jeremiah laughing in the background made him grind his teeth.

"Welcome home, mate," Jeremiah shouted.

There was a hush around them, and Kristoff's face warmed.

"Yes, welcome home, Alpha Mate Kristoff," a young voice said respectfully.

Kristoff smiled at the young man. His eyes were a blue Kristoff recognized immediately. Devin's son, Tarus. Had so much time passed that this young wolf was preparing to graduate high school? How much had he missed?

"Thank you, Tarus."

Tarus nodded respectfully. "We're glad to see you. Glad the alpha brought you home." A beat passed before he took up his argument again. "So, yeah. We want music, and no one agrees on the type."

Well, high school party-planner has apparently been added to the list of my duties now.

Hiring an official one would be the first item on his list the moment he could get everyone settled.

CHAPTER TWELVE

Jeremiah watched as Kristoff was dragged away by his people, those who'd been lost without his mate's guidance and support. Kristoff was a long way from his job as an assassin here in their home. It was a life Kristoff had left behind after coming to the compound, and one that made him a calmer man rather than the cold-blooded killer Jeremiah had first met. Kristoff was necessary here, and that had gone a long way to healing the emptiness he kept hidden inside.

Kristoff might have thrown Jeremiah some evil looks as one pack member held his hand and another reached for his elbow. But anyone could tell by merely looking that Kristoff was home.

Jeremiah finally had his touchstone, his foundation. As alpha, he wanted to be the one his people could seek in time of need, could connect to. It was a double-edged sword, because their numbers continued to grow. Being a leader of so many often made connecting an impossible task. He had relied on Kristoff, as his Second, to see their needs and act so he could focus on his other responsibilities.

They were a team, he and Kristoff, and he had been missing his key player both at his side and in his heart. But no longer.

Why had it taken him so long to realize the loss, to identify the bitter ache that overwhelmed him? No matter. Kristoff was his. He was here. And Jeremiah was never letting him go.

For now, Jeremiah had problems to resolve. Number one,

discovering Stefan's whereabouts. The man wanted something, and he needed to find out what that was. He would allow nothing and no one to disturb the mating he would share with Kristoff. None would take away the happiness he would finally claim.

His mate was home, his missing piece recovered. It was his job, his duty to his mate and his people, to do whatever he must to keep it that way. Yes, there would be missions Kristoff would need to partake in, but this would be where he returned. Always.

Jeremiah turned toward his house, searching for the son he'd left in charge. He smiled when it was a harrowed future alpha he found, riotous red curls struggling free from their binding. Wild eyes took him in, and a glorious smile filled with joy overtook Conner Tolliver's face.

He loved his son, was pleased he'd stepped in while Jeremiah had to be elsewhere, but he could tell Conner wasn't ready to fill his shoes. And perhaps Jeremiah wasn't quite ready to turn them over.

"Father! Praise unto the Goddess Moon, you're home." Conner did not hesitate to move from behind Jeremiah's desk, raking a hand through his hair. Conner's gaze shifted about with a quizzical expression. "Kristoff?"

"He's here."

"Ah," Conner gathered his jacket and his gun, along with his satchel and a few papers. "Happy for you, but even more so for me. My family needs me."

You have no idea how much, my son.

There was still the matter of a hyper-sexed sprite to see to, which Jeremiah was reluctant to tell his son about. He trusted Kristoff to handle it, and his son to blow a gasket.

"So, let's have an update on this," Jeremiah said.

"Yes. Then?" Conner questioned, his eyes on the exit before he respectfully refocused on Jeremiah.

"Then, I have a task for you."

"For me?"

"Yes, I have a feeling we're not quite done with Stefan, and I need this to end. Now. He's taken my mate's sanctuary, destroyed the home gifted to him by his sister. A treasure to have been passed on to his nephew, Peter."

Conner raised a brow. "You wanted him here. Without his home, he has no place else to go but here by your side."

Conner vexed him at times. Jeremiah had no doubt that if any obstacle stood between Conner and his wife or his children, the wolf wouldn't hesitate to locate the explosives that would destroy it.

"That's not what I want for him or for me, boy. I want this place to be his choice, the one he feels is his home no matter where he goes. Where we go."

Conner's eyes widened in alarm.

"Don't worry, you still get to play with your guns for now, but heed this. One day, you will take over as alpha of this pack, and someone else will need to shoulder the burden."

"Danny Boy?" Conner suggested eagerly.

Jeremiah snorted. His other son was human, a gift to him from his beautiful Sarai.

Could Danny lead the Iroquois Pack?

Jeremiah had to be honest. He hadn't considered the idea, but it was worth mulling over. It was funny. His Conner never saw Danny's humanity as a vulnerability. But then Danny wasn't weak. Had Danny not destroyed that sandman disguised as an abusive boyfriend? Danny's strength, coupled with the abilities of Aiden—a sandman Danny acted as *coimeádaí* for—could very well make their Danny Boy what the Iroquois Pack needed. He didn't miss the fact that it would give Conner what he needed as well. Freedom.

As for Jeremiah, he looked forward to traveling with his wayward mate, no hinderances or concerns. It wasn't that he didn't love the people he protected, but after so many years, he wanted a taste of that freedom Kristoff had enjoyed and the ability to share it with him.

As alpha, Jeremiah was first. He led his people, determined the outcome for a mother or a son or a father or a brother, someone, every day. He was both judge and jury, overseeing the success of his pack. He was the law to them, and they were the arm, carrying out his dictates, supporting the pack, and returning the love he gave tenfold.

Kristoff was his Second, his right hand, but Jeremiah craved more than that. He hungered to be first in Kristoff's heart. He needed to be the one person Kristoff counted on, the one he trusted to have his back, the one he wanted always by his side.

Jeremiah nodded. "We'll keep Danny in mind. No promises."

Conner coughed, no doubt trying to obscure the shout of joy he'd choked off.

Jeremiah decided to ignore it. "We have to look into Stefan's whereabouts."

"That's my area, Father. That's where I should be. On the field with my men hunting rather than trapped in this office shackled to a desk that still bears the scent of you and your mate." Conner looked at him with a twinkle in his eyes. "My arm, your law."

"See to it, then," Jeremiah bid and was surprised there weren't smoke trails from how quickly his son left the premises.

Jeremiah set his hands on his hips and turned around in his domain. Not much had changed since his absence. There was still the scent of coffee in the air — Mrs. Dunham's own brew. The curtains were open to allow the sun's sweet kiss. The desk itself was covered with papers in disarray, an indication of how stressed his son had been as he'd tried to cover for him in his absence. A difficult task, but it had been a necessary one.

Jeremiah walked behind his desk and sat in the empty chair. He turned toward the window to take in the view of the mountains in the distance, and closer, the gardens he loved so much. He remembered the times when he and Sarai had walked there, his arm protectively holding her close.

What would she think now of the love he kept in his heart for Kristoff? He chuckled to himself. She'd probably chide him for taking so long to drag the man he loved back home, to pull himself together and realize what Kristoff meant to him. Sarai had loved him and their sons. She had been the light to his darkness. When she'd died, taken away from them by cancer, Jeremiah had been tempted to follow her into the grave. It had been Mrs. Dunham's constant support, her strength, and demanding temperament that kept him tethered. Then later, it had been Kristoff who boosted his spirits.

How foolish I was to think otherwise? To believe I could survive without Kristoff?

When Kristoff had first left, Jeremiah had likened it to one of his missions. He would go and then return. He always had. But this time had been different. Months, then nearly a year, and would have been the beginnings of two if he hadn't received the call from Kristoff's former alpha.

Ha. Who am I fooling?

Jeremiah would not have made it another day, as he had already taken steps to search out his mate. The call had just given him a reason Kristoff might actually accept his presence.

No, Jeremiah had discovered how empty life was without Kristoff. And he would not have let another day pass before he would have him back again, in his arms where he belonged. Now, he only had to do what was necessary to keep him there.

The first step was to find Stefan. There was no question the worm had taken steps to destroy Kristoff's world, but to what purpose? If Stefan wanted Kristoff harmed, would he not be there to exact whatever punishment he'd been planning in his mind while he had been locked up for so many years? Why threaten the security Kristoff had developed in Charleston and then burn down his home?

What did he want? Revenge? Take away all Kristoff knew, destroy it?

Why not attack Kristoff himself rather than this subversive behavior?

"Ah, nice to have you home again, Alpha. Although, shouldn't you be with your lover rather than in this lonely office where Conner was held prisoner and the rest of us with him?"

Mrs. Dunham's sweet voice broke him from his thoughts. He loved the woman with all his heart. Had she not been there when Sarai died . . . He didn't want to think about it. Instead, he smiled at her warmly. The forest green sheath she wore over her generous figure complimented her auburn hair. She entered the room with tray in hand, a cup of tea for him and cakes of various sorts. He was hungry, he realized, but only when he scented the slivers of raw meat waiting on the tray did his mouth water.

"Kristoff?" he questioned.

"Has already been fed and watered and is taking a moment to deal with that wayward grandchild of yours. "

"You know?"

"Of course I know." Her gray eyes twinkled with humor. "The only ones blind to the machinations of that one are his distracted parental units. Shelly, with her ever-growing brood, and Conner, the warrior you were keeping shackled in this office while you secured your mate. If you had listened when I told you, Kristoff would never have left."

Jeremiah nodded his approval when Mrs. Dunham indicated more sugar.

As he drank, Jeremiah had to admit the older woman had

a point and had never been afraid to tell her alpha what was what, even when Jeremiah had been too stubborn and proud to listen. He wouldn't inform her of this, of course, never hungry enough to eat crow.

Mrs. Dunham placed her hand on his forearm and soothed him like the mother he'd lost an infinity ago. "Now, sit down and let me care of you, so you'll have the energy you'll need to chase after that mate of yours and claim him."

Jeremiah frowned, but Mrs. Dunham clucked at him, and he allowed himself to be guided behind his desk. Then Mrs. Dunham bustled to the front and removed the tray's lid. Jeremiah inhaled the deliciousness, his mouth watering, and his canines nearly dropping. The platter was filled with raw meat marinated with choice seasons and . . . what was it? Yellow dock? And nutmeg?

Ms. Dunham grinned slyly and handed him a napkin, which he settled on his lap. To his right, she placed a glass of liquid that smelled strongly of ginkgo biloba.

"You know, woman. I may be almost two hundred years old, but I am not without the potency of a hundred. These concoctions you have here will not help anything I don't already possess."

"Now, my Most Honored Alpha of the Iroquois Pack, Keeper of the Law, I have no doubt you will *rise* to the occasion, but what I have provided here couldn't hurt. Keep in mind you are preparing to capture one of the most feared wolves in the Northern Hemisphere. A little boost could only be advantageous."

Jeremiah shook his head and dug in. It was delicious, and besides, his dick was already hardening with the thought of having Kristoff beneath him.

"What's in this?"

"A little of this. A bit of that. We would simply like to do what is necessary to speed along the process and make sure it sticks."

Jeremiah shook his head. The woman would kill him with her directness. Mrs. Dunham wasn't one to mince words or leave her audience guessing. She was a constant in his life and had been a blessing while he waited for Kristoff to return.

"Regardless, I don't need a blue pill or any of those human drugs to enhance my ability to care for my mate." Jeremiah's bracelets jingled as he picked up another sliver of meat, moaning when the flavor danced along his tongue. Groaning in pleasure, he downed three more pieces hungrily, the savory spices an orgasmic sensation.

"Ah, now that look you have, the one where your beast is fighting from within? Your beast is eager to hunt its prey and rip the meat from its bones. That's the one we'll be needing to see ravaging that mate of yours."

Jeremiah dug in and relished his meal, the wolf in him awakened, as Mrs. Donovan had indicated, by the blood-rich morsels. Jeremiah would devour this, and then they would find their mate.

CHAPTER THIRTEEN

Stefan watched the Iroquois Pack encampment from his vantage point. They'd had to travel miles outside of Louisville and nearly drove off the bend of several roads until they'd arrived at a lush green land populated with homes. A few large ranch styles spotted the area while others varied from two-story buildings to small cottages. The largest one was up a hill, but still close enough to monitor the people surrounding it. It was vast, with a huge garden at the back, and balconies at almost every window. He'd have called it a mansion, but it looked more like a home that belonged in another world, another time. Almost like a castle with ancient brick and high walls.

Ireland?

There had to be more than twenty rooms, and with the many people he'd seen enter and exit, it wasn't just one family residing there. Stefan knew that was where Jeremiah Tolliver lived, and where he was, Kristoff had to be.

This was a small obstacle, one he and the wolves he'd brought with him could overcome.

He only needed to speak to Kristoff, show him what he'd begun for them. He would present the pack he was grooming for them, the one they would lead together, combined with the dregs of the Iroquois Pack once they'd killed its current alpha and his family. Remove any challengers, and it would all belong to them. Well, him first, of course.

After all, Kristoff, no matter how dangerous he appeared to others, was ruled by his heart. If not, he would have killed

Stefan, not placed him somewhere he could learn his secrets and discover the path that would eventually reunite them.

Kristoff wouldn't have submitted to Jeremiah, who lorded his alpha status over him. Jeremiah used it as a way to make Kristoff grovel, and Kristoff should never have to bow to anyone unless it was to Stefan. He knew how to take care of Kristoff, how to show him his worth.

No, Stefan had done the right thing. He'd spooked that old bitch and chased her off. He'd visited the cunt basket weaver, and she'd taken a much-needed vacation. It would have been easier to kill them, but he wanted Kristoff vulnerable, not broken. No, he'd saved the house for that. He could always dangle the women as an incentive if necessary.

Kristoff's home had been a significant sacrifice, the one that would make him ready for Stefan. Only Jeremiah had gotten there first.

Everything happens for a reason. Stefan chose to see it that way, at least. This pack and everything that went with it, the money, the land, and its resources, would be theirs. It was meant to be.

Stefan drew his hand down to his crotch, squeezing his rigid cock. "Soon, Kristoff."

At first, the idea of mating Kristoff had not appealed. Stefan loved the tender curves of women, their cries of pleasure and then pain when he took them.

But he'd been practicing and found a man's tight hole could be just as sweet and tender. He'd picked up a few strays from a club here or there, men no one would miss. He was careful, not killing the first two or three, but then it had been too difficult to resist the role as giver of life and death. More often, he chose death. The scent of their blood when he'd fucked his way to orgasm provided completion. Their vulnerability, and his need for their fear, brought him the pleasure he was helpless to resist.

They didn't matter anymore. He had wolves now. Stefan learned they could bleed, their essence drenching the sheets on which they lay, and still thrive.

They healed. They could survive to be retaken, fucked, ripped apart, and they would repair themselves. Iron in the lube he used to ready their holes, some in the food he fed them, and they were weak enough to enjoy the kind of fucking Stefan desired.

The ones he'd been given as playthings were young, yes, as tender as he required. They were more youthful than Kristoff, whom he'd learned was over a hundred. His factfinders had been fruitful in their research. He wondered about the age of the alpha. Someone that attracted the submission of others, who men and women would die for, had to have lived centuries. The power of an alpha led to greatness.

There had to be a way to acquire that power, to possess that energy, to harness that life for himself. Hadn't Stefan read stories where men were turned into wolves? With a creature as strong as Kristoff, anything was possible. Long life, wealth, and power, the three things he craved.

As for Kristoff, he would be beautiful in his pain.

"The money," a deep baritone questioned.

"Will be wired into your account the moment I have him. As promised."

Money was a motivating force few could ignore. He'd lured this pack to him with the promise of enough to care for their hungry bitches, feed their young, and live above all the other packs they envied. The enticement had been like salmon to a grizzly for them. They hadn't hesitated in sharing their young and weak, those without protectors, for his pleasure.

He used them to his greatest desire. He relished the flick of his knife against their pulsing veins, making them shiver and his dick harden.

It was a powerful feeling, and one never sated. Stefan

hoped to share this with Kristoff. To have Kristoff's dominance, his iron will under his control, would be a heady gift for him.

"What of the security?" Stefan inquired.

"It's nothing. Just have the money as agreed. These will be easy kills."

This male was arrogant, perhaps too arrogant. Stefan would make sure he was one of the first to go.

After he'd used him, of course.

CHAPTER FOURTEEN

K ristoff walked toward the property he'd known as his while he lived on Iroquois Pack lands. He had no idea what the state of the building would be. Often, when he'd traveled before, he'd returned to find the ranch home with the lights on, the rooms warm and prepared for his arrival. Other times, when he'd been absent for months, the house had been locked up but was still clean and habitable when he returned, no dust or cobwebs to be found. Of course, Mrs. Dunham was to be thanked for that.

He and Jeremiah had traveled for hours before arriving earlier that day only for him to be waylaid by teenagers and well-meaning adults with their own versions of what a senior graduation party should entail. Thankfully he'd been able to procure a party-planner, someone more skilled at event planning for teens and who actually enjoyed what he thought of as a nightmare. He'd rather be tortured than pick a DJ, could care less about selecting the theme for the evening, and he had no interest in deciding finger foods. After Carson Nightengale arrived, a vibrant creature with plans galore, Kristoff had made his escape.

Later, Kristoff rescued a sexed-out human still being devoured by Jeremiah's grandson. Seeing Samuel's dick buried deep inside the man, Kristoff had threatened to bring in reinforcements, mainly Samuel's human keeper and best friend, Darren. Darren was on a case out of town, and per usual, Samuel had gone AWOL. It was an odd relationship between the two of them, but Kristoff had ceased to question it. He employed the threat of Darren to get Samuel to finally behave. Samuel was formidable, a minx who feasted on sexual energy. The little monster was a handful, but it couldn't be helped, given his parentage.

Kristoff had called Darren, who promised he would return soon.

For now, he had everything under control, and Samuel was back at his studies. He had to wonder if Samuel's most recent actions were not the cry for attention they appeared to be. Unfortunately, the memory of Samuel's constant promises to be good if Kristoff stayed played like a broken record in his brain.

"If you had remembered to come home instead of forgetting you're like another parent to us all, then maybe wayward humans wouldn't find their way to my bed," the man-child said, his hands twisting the hair of the human he held close to him. The human only looked up, his big blue eyes gazing at Samuel adoringly, ready to do his bidding.

"I . . ."

"Ran away. That's what you did, and you left us to fend for ourselves. My grandfather is your mate. You should have claimed his ass as yours years ago, and this would never have happened."

"You will not blame your predilections on me."

"Nope. Just the fact you weren't here to stop me." Samuel sighed deeply when the human's hands climbed over his skin, on a determined journey directed toward his cock.

"You're home now. Let's keep it that way." After that, Samuel had kissed the man profoundly and handed him over. "There you go, sweetheart. Kristoff will make sure you get home. Uncle Aiden's not here to help you forget, so perhaps we'll see each other again. You know, maybe at a class or two?" Samuel's dark green eyes glanced at Kristoff with hope, but he sighed tragically when he received no response. "Well, maybe not. Bye now."

Kristoff growled as he pushed the human toward Brandon, one of his assistants. "Your ass — "

"Needs Darren's hands, but he's busy." After a yawn, which was obviously for show, Samuel waved him off and curled into bed, feigning sleep.

Kristoff shook his head and nodded to Brandon, who smiled. "Welcome home, Alpha Mate Kristoff."

"Thank you, I think."

In the end, the human, whose name was Jonathan, had been situated. Aiden was called because even if Samuel forgot, Kristoff did not. Aiden could wipe memories continents away. He was a sandman, after all. So, showered fresh and well-fed, the young man had been dropped off at his dorm with no memory of the encounter.

And now Kristoff was ready to kick back in his home, perhaps have a cup of tea — one of the ones he'd taken from Mrs. Hilliard's home at her request. Hopefully, they'd delivered his meager belongings there.

But when he arrived, he was surprised to see cars in the driveway that didn't belong to him, a garishly decorated flag blowing in the wind, children chasing each other in the yard, and two adoring fathers watching them play.

"Alpha Mate Kristoff," the older one said with a nod.

"Liam." He wanted to ask the man why he was here, how he had made himself comfortable in a home that belonged to someone else, but there were three sets of eyes watching him apprehensively.

"Yes, sir. We would like to thank you for allowing us to live here." *Ah, Jeremiah.* "The children have adjusted to life here. The people have been nothing but kind, and we're grateful. The alpha said you wouldn't mind."

Of course, Jeremiah had. All the better to limit Kristoff's options.

Kristoff looked around and saw the house had indeed become a home, complete with flowers decorating the wraparound porch, the scattering of toys on the ground, and a boy and girl who raced toward him with their arms wide open.

Misha and Rook. He'd rescued the two from a human trafficking ring, one that hadn't realized they'd stolen pups. The mother lost, it had been a blessing to find their uncle and their uncle's mate hoping for a family of their own.

He held the two little ones to him and sighed. So much ugliness in the world. He was grateful to see when he'd accomplished something good like bringing together this family. They were here now, all of them, and safe.

That was what mattered.

"Well, I wondered where my mate had gotten to."

Kristoff shivered as he let the two little ones go to resume their game of chase. Jeremiah's scent permeated the air, and Kristoff's entire body reacted to his closeness. The jingle of Jeremiah's bracelets reached his ears as a hand was placed at the small of his back. "I've come to bring you home, Kristoff. I could wait no longer."

Kristoff had been fooling himself to believe he could ever say no to Jeremiah Tolliver. He turned to him then, confident his heart was in his eyes, his submission easily read.

Kristoff wanted . . . craved his alpha. He was done running, done living a lie. He would have knelt right at Jeremiah's feet if the man did not grip him tightly at his elbow, his sharp teeth lowering at the scent of Kristoff's submission.

"My love."

"Please," Kristoff demanded. He hungered, the need slicing through his soul and cleaving him in two. His wolf could take no more, and Kristoff was in agreement with his beast as it longed to mate with its alpha.

"Alpha, we are surprised to see you and your mate here. It was nice of you to visit, for we are always grateful, but we thought you'd be home" — Misha paused, glancing around for tiny listening ears—"resting."

Jeremiah laughed knowingly. "It would seem I neglected to inform my mate that I have readied our home for his welcome." There was no way to mistake the hunger in Jeremiah's voice, the want that echoed his own.

Jeremiah had changed clothes at some point, replacing his travel clothes with a snug pair of dark jeans and a Henley wrapped around his muscles in a way that made Kristoff's mouth water. His long hair had lost its thong and lay in waves over his broad shoulders.

Kristoff loved Jeremiah's hair, had brushed his fingers over it twice that he could remember. Now, he wanted to wrap the length around his fist and pull the man toward him, devour him with a kiss that would leave no questions as to what he wanted next. He yearned to claim his mate and to be claimed. He wanted Jeremiah's length deep inside him where no other had ever been, for Jeremiah to possess him.

Jeremiah's dark eyes caught the light from the waning sun, and Kristoff felt the kiss of their touch along his skin. Jeremiah hungered for him, and Kristoff welcomed it.

"It's getting late, and I would like for us to be home where I can see to my mate's needs," his alpha said, his gaze locked on him.

Yes, that. See to my needs, especially the rock-hard length of my cock.

"Certainly, alpha. It's good to see you home along with your mate," Liam said.

When had everyone accepted this bond between me and Jeremiah?

Kristoff hadn't been here in almost a year. Yet as he'd walked through the compound, he'd been greeted as the alpha's mate by so many. Had there been a pack meeting? Had Jeremiah informed their people of his desire? Of the commitment between the two of them the alpha had ignored for so many years?

There were things they needed to talk about, to discuss, but all Kristoff could think about was riding Jeremiah's dick. The waves of pheromones coming off Jeremiah were affecting Kristoff's brain cells. Any longer and he'd help Jeremiah by ripping the clothes away from his body.

"Yes, we can certainly understand," Misha added. "Now that you're back, Kristoff, we'd like to talk to you about college tours. The alpha mentioned you'd be able to help organize these."

"Yes, tours," Kristoff agreed, his mind only half on the conversation. He was more interested in what Jeremiah's seed tasted like as his alpha watched him, his lips curving in a smile. "For now, I'll leave you and arrange something another day." *There, that should appease these two so Jeremiah and I can go fuck.*

"Of course," the mates said in unison.

Kristoff sighed with pleasure when Jeremiah wrapped his arm around his shoulders, pulling him close as they walked away. "There you are, my sweet one. Let me take care of you. Love you. You're home now, and your wolf recognizes this, recognizes me. No more running unless it is to our bed."

CHAPTER FIFTEEN

Jeremiah could scent the submission on Kristoff's skin and was too eager to enjoy the gift to remain at his mate's former dwelling. No, he'd given that house away the moment Kristoff left. There hadn't been much of Kristoff's to move from the place. His wolf had never truly lived there, a nomad of sorts. Kristoff's home was now at Jeremiah's side.

In the past, Kristoff had rarely been absent from Jeremiah's side. He had often stayed at the main house in a guest room when there had so much to do, when it had been more convenient for him to spend the night. Only at times when he had gotten frustrated and angry did Kristoff seek his own place to be where he could reset and be what Jeremiah needed. Jeremiah had known of Kristoff's cravings. He had shared them but had chosen to ignore them.

Those days were over now. Now, Kristoff would not only live in Jeremiah's home as he should be, but he would sleep beside Jeremiah in *their* bed. Jeremiah planned to love Kristoff and fuck him until he was too exhausted to do anything but collapse in his arms.

"When?" Kristoff grumbled as the two of them turned toward their home.

Jeremiah didn't have to ask. He knew Kristoff referred to what had once been his house. He held tightly to Kristoff's hand, the knowledge the man could let go and walk away ever-present in his mind. He'd never make that mistake again, never give Kristoff a reason to believe he wasn't vital to him, and to the pack. Kristoff thought he'd failed them. But no, it was he who had failed Kristoff.

But now? Kristoff was Jeremiah's completely. He would never give him up.

"The moment you left, I gave the house to them. You'd brought them home, and they needed a place to stay."

"But I lived there."

"Yes, you did, but that was never truly your home."

Kristoff nodded, and Jeremiah smiled at his mate's agreement. He could do nothing else.

They soon arrived at the home the two would share for as long as the Goddess Moon granted them.

Jeremiah loved his home, built centuries ago to accommodate him and his growing pack as well as his mate and children. The wraparound porch, the trellises, and the verandah made the home quaint. And then there were the parts added on, which resembled the sprawling castles he remembered from childhood. It was a sanctuary for the families that lived there, the house easily fitting them all.

His sons had moved away with their families to different parts of the territory now. His grandchildren, the army of young ones Connor continued to add to, multiplied and needed space, some even living in their own homes.

Danny Boy and his mate, Aiden, had traveled off with Peter and Remi to meet the members of Peter's pack in Russia. They'd wanted to show a united front, one that had overcome their diversity.

This meant, for now, it was just Jeremiah, Mrs. Dunham, Samuel, one of the vampires he fostered, and now Kristoff. There were always others who would show up for meals. Mrs. Dunham's cooking was too irresistible to be ignored. And whenever necessary, the pack would gather for meetings, or when they needed each other's company. So while his children and grandchildren lived away, there were nights and even weeks when they returned to stay in the residence.

Regardless, he would fuck Kristoff on every flat surface of his three-story home, in every one of the bedrooms, both kitchens, and the gardens. Yes, in the gardens beside every rose bush and all the flowers and plants he had no names for as they were the prizes of his beautiful Sarai. Now they would be place markers for where he showed Kristoff how much he loved his body, his spirit, and his wolf.

Jeremiah would mark Kristoff as his own. His canines were already dropping with the idea. He took a deep breath to regain his control.

"No," Kristoff conceded. "It wasn't."

"I was and am your home, my wolf. Your things, what little you have now, are here, in this house, your possessions in our bedroom. Your weapons will be replaced and secured here. And your art? There is a studio here now where you can paint and draw and even basket weave, anything you wish. I called ahead and asked that everything be made ready. I wanted it all perfect for you. The only thing missing is us between the sheets. I plan to remedy that immediately."

Kristoff's smile was slow, his eyes glistening while Jeremiah spoke.

"Home."

"Yes, Kristoff. You are home, you are mine, and I will never let you go again."

Jeremiah stood at the end of the bed, Kristoff, his silver-haired wolf, stretched out before him, his sculpted body waiting for Jeremiah to mark, savor, and possess.

The way Kristoff had glanced around the home as if he'd never seen it before made Jeremiah's heart swell. He'd had pictures of Kristoff's childhood home in Russia brought in, had rooms decorated in Kristoff's earthy tones—ones he knew the man loved. He had secured art pieces he knew Kristoff would appreciate and added them to the walls, as well as various woven baskets placed on a table here or there throughout the house.

Jeremiah's bedroom had been remodeled to suit two men, including large sofas and a wall of books he knew Kristoff enjoyed. He had added an easel to the room complete with the paints, crayons, and charcoal he knew Kristoff would utilize.

As much as Jeremiah could, he'd made this room theirs. He'd even replaced the bed with a larger framed one and found himself imagining tying Kristoff to it with soft leather straps wrapped around his thick wrists. He wanted his mate pleading when he possessed him, writhing in passion and unable to experience anything but pleasure.

It was a fantasy he'd had too often to count, and now he could make it their reality.

Jeremiah craved his mate, needed him, and now he would have him. Nothing would hold him back. Nothing and no one, especially himself.

There would be no more hesitations, no recriminations from the past, no fears of the human still out there waiting for his chance to attack.

No, this time was theirs.

"Come to me," Jeremiah growled, his claws nearly piercing his flesh. His beast was just beneath the surface, and he no longer wanted to hold him back. They both deserved this moment.

Kristoff's green eyes flashed, the heat from them enough to melt a candle. "What would you have of me, my alpha? Would you like me to kneel at your feet, beg for your touch?"

Jeremiah's skin itched with the need to drag his mate to him, but it had to be Kristoff's choice, his decision. "I want you any way you'll let me have you, Kristoff. I need you more than air to breathe. Your touch alone would send me up in flames, and yet I crave the inferno. But I will not take you. This, what we have?" Jeremiah waved his hand between the two of them, the bangles he wore chiming on his wrist. Each piece was a memory of the battles he'd left behind, carried names of those lost. The battle he fought now was against himself, one with his mate as the spoils. "This must be your decision. I must be your choice. What do you say, mate of mine, *mo grá?*"

Jeremiah watched the struggle on Kristoff's face and knew he remembered the times Jeremiah had denied him, choosing to live in the past rather than accept the gift Kristoff offered as a future.

"And if I choose this, choose you, then what?" Kristoff's voice was soft, simultaneously tinged with fear and hope.

"Then you and I will live eternity together, loving one another, fighting at each other's side. I will love you forever as I do now, my wolf. I would worship the bond we share and show you, each and every day, how grateful I am for the opportunity to love you, and for you loving me." Jeremiah prayed Kristoff could hear the truth in his words.

Jeremiah saw it then, the love reflected in Kristoff's eyes, the fire they both shared. Only one more step. That was all he needed. He tightened his fists until he knew he'd drawn blood. He would wait until it killed him for his mate's response.

"I do," Kristoff said, his body close enough to touch now. He reached up, his hand running through Jeremiah's hair, making him sigh in pleasure. "I love you, have for so many years. I thought it would finally kill me if I couldn't have you."

"You can now and forever, my love. I'm here. Yours to take, to love. I need you," Jeremiah gasped when Kristoff struck, sharp teeth biting into the flesh of his throat. His wolf howled deep within, eager to slam their mate on the nearest flat surface and take what belonged to them. Finally.

"My wolf is beginning to question your ownership, alpha,"

Kristoff taunted, rolling his hips as he pressed against Jeremiah's body.

"That should never happen, mate. Your wolf should always know the keeper of his soul." Jeremiah growled before wrapping his arm around Kristoff's waist and throwing his mate to the bed. "Your wolf should know its alpha, should never question who its master is."

Kristoff groaned, and Jeremiah's dick, already hard as steel, was slick with need and ready to take what was his. They'd touched and kissed. But those were mere samples of what he wanted to do to his lover. Claim him. Love him. Make him his forever. Be Kristoff's in return, always. That was what Jeremiah yearned for desperately.

"Show me," Kristoff begged.

Jeremiah could hold back no longer. His claws exploded from his fingertips, and his canines lengthened, ready to sink into Kristoff's flesh.

"There you are, my alpha, my mate." Kristoff's smile teased as he reached inside his pants to yank them down over his ample bottom. Then he gripped his hard dick with his fist and tugged.

Jeremiah's mouth watered. "So sweet, the way you play with yourself. Show me how you like it, my mate, how you like that delicious cock of yours handled. I want to learn what pleases you so I can do it better and drive you out of your mind."

The effect Jeremiah's words had on Kristoff was incredible to watch. The way Kristoff's green eyes darkened when he reached behind himself to open up his hole, giving Jeremiah a peek of dark furled flesh. It made him want to eat his own words right after he ate Kristoff's ass.

Jeremiah knelt on the bed and inhaled the scent of Kristoff's heat. Opening his mouth, he allowed Kristoff to feed him his dick. He drew his tongue along the thick veins and swallowed deep. Kristoff's cries were loud, his pants a symphony, and Jeremiah loved it all, demanding an encore.

"So much, my alpha. *Blyad*. Fuck. I have dreamed of this moment, prayed for it. How do I know you won't take it away, leave me hungry and starving in the street, desperate for your taste?"

Kristoff's scream of pain was loud enough to shake the walls of the bedroom when Jeremiah struck. Jeremiah feasted on his mate's blood, the taste delicious on his tongue, a flavor he would never have to remember for it would be with him always. He drank and swallowed, relishing his mate's vulnerability as Kristoff submitted.

Kristoff's breaths were labored and his movements slow as Jeremiah took what he needed.

When Jeremiah lifted his head, he knew his eyes were black, the pupils blown. His skin was feverish with his wolf's need to capture his mate's essence.

When Kristoff whispered his name, his voice shallow and weak, Jeremiah's smile was slow, and he knew he was too far gone. He was more animal than man. He lifted above Kristoff and used claws to shred the rest of his expensive clothing until all that was left was ivory skin waiting for Jeremiah's touch.

"When I take you, my mate, you will exist on the planes between life and death. I will bring you back, body and soul. I will venture into your mind, into every crevice of your being, and claim you entirely."

Jeremiah pulled Kristoff's legs open wide and dipped low, inhaling the scent of his inner core. He tasted and licked and savored the mewls and whimpers his overcome mate made. Using Kristoff's blood and his own saliva, he stretched Kristoff open, not wanting the first time he plunged into his mate to rip him apart.

"I need," Kristoff said, his voice rough with desire.

"I know, *mo grá*, my love. It is time for us to become one.

First, in body, then in soul. We shall never be apart." Jeremiah spread Kristoff's legs wider and centered himself between them, pointing his hungry cock toward home. "Now, for your body." Jeremiah didn't waste time. Kristoff was prepared, more than ready for his alpha to surge within his depths, and Jeremiah roared with pleasure. Thrusting forward, he rammed his rod inside the heat of Kristoff's body, celebrating the cries his lover made. Kristoff's roar was even louder as he pleaded for more, shouting each time Jeremiah impaled his body and bottoming out.

"Sweet, sweet mate. So strong, so powerful, striking fear in monster and human. Indestructible. Completely mine. Subject to my needs, my wants, and mine for the taking." Jeremiah punctuated each word with thrusts into Kristoff's body.

"Jeremiah," Kristoff moaned. "*Moya lyubov.*"

"Kristoff, yes, I am your love. I am your alpha, your mate eternally." Jeremiah's next thrust shoved Kristoff against the headboard. When Kristoff screamed for more, Jeremiah worked hard to deliver. Kristoff was at Jeremiah's mercy. He had the taste of his blood on his tongue, his dick deep in his ass, and his mind ready and open to Jeremiah's claiming.

"More," Kristoff shouted.

It was all Jeremiah needed. He rose, unsheathing himself from Kristoff's hole. In seconds, he had his love face down, his ass in the air, and plunged into him once again. "So good."

Kristoff needed pain, needed to know he was owned, that he was safe. His lover hungered for grounding. Too often, Kristoff's needs were forgotten when others saw him only as a weapon, his chilly demeanor and icy visage never giving away the soul beneath. Jeremiah saw him, loved him. They were made for each other, and Jeremiah intended to show his mate this was permanent. What they had was real, and he was never letting go.

And with that, he entered his mate's mind.

Chapter Sixteen

Kristoff was overwhelmed, his sensations chaotic and impossible to assess. He was impaled on the end of Jeremiah's cock, his body subject to his mate. Jeremiah had drunk from him, leaving him hungry and needy, his body enflamed, and still, he hung on the precipice of something greater, more.

It was all too much and not enough.

Kristoff was in the arms of the man he loved, a man he had often prayed would accept him, accept their bond. And now he had it but was unsure. He was afraid and didn't know if what Jeremiah seemed to finally embrace would last.

Mine.

The word whispered along the tendrils of his mind, invading his psyche while Jeremiah invaded his body. Jeremiah was everywhere, surrounding him, inside him, a part of him, and he moaned with the pleasure.

Mate.

This time, the word was accompanied by a growl, and Kristoff acknowledged Jeremiah's wolf, his own wolf answering. If he shifted, he would be belly up, submitting to his alpha. Instead, he was in a sensual euphoria welcoming any and everything Jeremiah had to give.

Yes. You are mine, body and soul, my love forever and always.

Kristoff could feel Jeremiah's sincerity, feel the honesty inside his own mind. Jeremiah was a part of him now, had entered his thoughts, had made him vulnerable so that he lacked the strength to thrust him out, to keep him out. Right here, right now, Kristoff knew his mate's words to be true. They were one. They were united, and they were forever.

Kristoff laughed loudly when Jeremiah flipped him again. Here he was, knowledgeable in various martial arts, could master any weapon, and had so many kills he'd lost count, yet his alpha made him feel small. And, fuck it, Kristoff loved it.

He moaned when Jeremiah nuzzled at his neck again, drawing his tongue along the skin where his sharp canines had met.

Take from me, Jeremiah whispered in his mind. *Accept me. My arm your law.*

No. Not as my beta. Not as my soldier. Not as my right arm. Take from me as your mate, as your lover, as the keeper of your heart.

Flames licked along Kristoff's skin, and his own canines fell, the incisors wickedly sharp. He was careful not to run his tongue across them, as he'd cut himself that way many times. He looked up then.

Do you see me, mate? Jeremiah's voice caressed his mind.
I do.

Do you accept our bond?
I do.

Jeremiah smiled then, and in seconds Jeremiah lay flat on his back, his dick still buried in Kristoff's ass, his palms holding him still while his fingers drew tiny circles on his flesh.

Jeremiah stretched his neck, inviting Kristoff to take a bite.
Take from me, allow yourself sustenance. Be full and be mine.

Kristoff growled, his wolf not sharing his hesitation. He lowered until he was able to press his nose against Jeremiah's warm neck.

"I can hear your heart beating, the way it races for me. I want to paint you this way, ready for me, welcoming me. I want to show the world the way your eyes shine when you look at me, the love I see there. I want them to see the smile that belongs to me and me alone." He sniffed along Jeremiah's skin, grunting as Jeremiah's swollen member shifted slightly.

Kristoff sighed and rolled his hips, loving Jeremiah's gasps.

"I wish I could paint the naughty sounds you make, so dirty." He opened his mouth wide against the vein that pulsed beneath tender flesh. His wolf was so beautiful, so precious. The scent of his skin tantalizing in a way nothing else could be made his canines drop.

Jeremiah growled and fucked his mate, rammed his iron-hard dick inside Kristoff's tight ass, loving the cries he made. He spread Kristoff's cheeks with the palms of his hands and ran his fingertips along his dick as it invaded Kristoff's hole.

The blood was warm, the way it flowed over his tongue pleasure beyond measure. Entirely his in every way. Jeremiah moaned, savoring the taste as he pulled his mate's legs wide.

"Mine," Jeremiah roared, the joy of claiming his mate too high to contain.

"Yours, my alpha. *Lyubov moya.*"

"Your alpha, your love, and your mate."

"My mate," Kristoff shouted as Jeremiah pulled Kristoff to him, held him tight while he fucked his lover. The two of them came together, Jeremiah's seed flooding Kristoff's hole. Kristoff's dick spurt streams of cum over Jeremiah's hot flesh.

It wasn't enough to fuck Kristoff. Jeremiah wanted Kristoff to feel his presence everywhere, in his body, his mind. Jeremiah was only too eager to retake him this time against a wall, his dick thrust inside him, slick with their come. He roared before slamming his canines into Kristoff's throat once more, lapping at the blood there.

"I've waited a lifetime for this," Kristoff gasped, his heart racing beneath Jeremiah's palm, his claws pressing against the tender flesh there. "More. Give me all of you."

Jeremiah moaned, "Every day, *a chroí.*"

"Your heart," Kristoff sighed in question, his cheek against Jeremiah's shoulder. When his mate lifted his head up, his face was no longer human. He was more wolf than man.

"My heart," Jeremiah growled, the voice more a roar than actual words.

Jeremiah picked up Kristoff, Kristoff's dick hard and long, bouncing in the air, and took him down to the floor, slamming his way home.

"Not enough. Never enough," Kristoff groaned, tears at his cheeks as he was driven across the floor with Jeremiah's thrusts. He screamed when Jeremiah's claws sank into his thighs to keep him in place.

"Jeremiah!"

"Fucking stay, *a ghra*, my love. Never leave again." Jeremiah needed Kristoff to understand. If he didn't believe the words, the walk he'd taken in his mind, then maybe his body would speak for him. It was urgent to him, necessary that Kristoff accepted his place in Jeremiah's life, in their world, that he never again seek another home elsewhere. This was his home. Jeremiah was his home, where he belonged.

Once again, Jeremiah emptied himself into his mate, smiling when he both heard and felt Kristoff release beneath him.

They lay together then, coated in each other's seed, sticky and sated.

Jeremiah tightened his arms around Kristoff and nipped at his ear. "Again."

"Yes, my alpha."

Later, Jeremiah was able to get them both onto the bed, the scent of their lovemaking surrounding them. His wolf was pleased with the taking of their mate and the total dominance of it all. Kristoff, often spoken of in terrifying whispers in the dark, the boogeyman of the Iroquois Pack, slept safe and at peace within the circle of Jeremiah's arms, his face in the crook of Jeremiah's neck. It was all that Jeremiah had ever dreamed when he'd finally realized who he needed and had so foolishly let go.

Never again.

He would lock him away if he had to. Indeed, Kristoff could find a way out, but by then, Jeremiah would have fucked his lover into such a stupor, escape with be a fleeting thought.

He bent and kissed Kristoff's lips softly, enjoyed the flavor of his own seed on his mate. He dipped his tongue within, savoring the sweetness, and moaned when Kristoff's tongue flirted with his, Kristoff's green eyes opening to look at him with warmth.

"Inside you," Jeremiah whispered when he pulled back.

"It's a good thing my ass can heal so swiftly." Kristoff's snark was quickly cut off by Jeremiah's questing fingers.

"Feels ready to me." Jeremiah lifted his fingers to his mouth, fingers that had just spread Kristoff's well-used hole wide open, and licked them.

Kristoff moaned with pleasure and welcomed his mate.

The night passed with tender touches and kisses sliding into hard and rough brushes with bruises and marks Kristoff treasured. He couldn't believe he was finally where he needed to be, held by the wolf he loved, by his alpha. He savored the licks along his neck. Kristoff hungered for the caresses at his waist. He loved the way Jeremiah held him close as if afraid to let him go. Kristoff could feel it in the way Jeremiah held him against his heart, his legs wrapped around Kristoff's, his way of ensuring his mate stayed where he belonged.

Kristoff didn't offer any promises, didn't give any oaths to remain there forever. Words weren't necessary. His submission was there in the way he moved closer to Jeremiah, notched his head beneath his alpha's chin, and slept in the safety of his arms.

Kristoff was home.

CHAPTER SEVENTEEN

Time had passed, and Kristoff's life with Jeremiah had reached a sort of rhythm, a soundtrack filled with caring for the pack, breakfasts together, evening runs, and lovemaking late into the night. Kristoff was never bored. This was life for him now, a life where pack members came to ask for his advice and left behind a savory treat or gift. They laughed with him, showing him pictures of their young and including him in events. Kristoff had a family here.

Kristoff always had his nephew. It was one of the original reasons he'd chosen to stay at the compound, for Peter's protection, but now he cared for the pack as if it were his own. And it was. He was the alpha's mate, and that meant a great deal to the people here who sought the alpha's protection and favor. Jeremiah was content, his heart settled, and this made his people happy. In turn, they wanted to keep his mate happy as well.

It was surprising to Kristoff that he no longer thought of the next mission or polished his guns nightly. Instead, he worked with his oils and his pastels. He painted the Belle of Louisville from the perspective he and Jeremiah had enjoyed the week before. He had actually begun a class with the little ones at their school. Kristoff the big bad assassin weaving baskets. Mary would be proud of him. The few he'd made had turned out nicely, not as beautifully detailed as hers perhaps, but close enough. The young pups had taken to the craft and were pleased to take something home to their parents as gifts. He'd done that, passed along an artform he'd come to love.

Kristoff wanted more. And he could have it. No, he wasn't bored. How could he be? His plate was more than full. It was overflowing. Ensuring a place for their youth to grow and experience life beyond the compound, maintaining the businesses the pack chartered, and supplementing his alpha's leadership were enough to keep him busy. Add to that the tumultuous Samuel, who needed *his Darren* to come home, and there was no need to find the darkness. It would find its way here.

"Have you reached Darren," a warm voice called from the pantry

"Yes. He should be on a flight home tomorrow afternoon."

"It's a good thing, that." Mrs. Dunham pushed her way into the kitchen, hands filled with freshly made bread. The scent of cinnamon and nutmeg teased Kristoff's nose, and the drop of Russian whiskey she'd added to his tea on the kitchen island had him rising from his seat to give her a hand.

"Shoo, I've got this, my boy. I've been handling dishes and the like far longer than you've been alive. I've my own bit of information for you, alpha mate."

"Do you?" Kristoff asked.

"Yes, love. I do. Your friend, Mrs. Hilliard, is doing well, and after a bit of talking, she finds the thought of the supernatural world not so fearsome. She plans to visit in a few weeks. I liked her. Seems she and I have a lot in common, much of that being our love for a certain stalwart wolf who felt he could trudge through life unfettered and unloved. Good to know we've both laid waste to that myth, now." She set the tray down and bent to turn on the oven.

Kristoff shook his head and leaned back against the counter, laughing softly. The woman was nothing if not straight to the point. No wondering or double entendre. It was why he loved her, and perhaps why he loved Mrs. Hilliard as well. Kristoff hadn't had time for mothering when he was younger, at least not that he could remember. Weapons, that was what his childhood held. A mother's touch was a memory that eluded him.

Kristoff picked up the cup before him and sipped. "This is delicious, Mrs. Donovan. Thank you."

"Oh, pah," she said, but her cheeks reddened. "I'm glad there was a good woman, someone that I am grateful to for watching over you when you ran away."

"Yes, she did do that."

"It was nice, yes? Having a family, having someone notice when you're gone."

"I can notice when I'm gone. I can take care of myself." The woman was after something, hence the baiting. Kristoff was confident he wouldn't have to wait long to see what that was.

"And no one questions that, my boy." Mrs. Dunham smiled at him, the light catching in her cerulean eyes. "I question your ability to realize how much you're valued here."

She was wrong there. Kristoff realized his worth the mornings when people invited him into their homes, depended on him, and made him a significant part of their lives.

"Just the other day, I know you spoke to young Peter, giving him advice." Mrs. Dunham nodded in his direction, encouraging him to share.

"Yes, I spoke to him. The governing of his new coven is not without bumps and divots, but there has been progress made."

"This is good. So now, what next?"

"I don't know what you mean."

"Seems to me you two have decided to accept your mating bond, which is good. Still, the pack deserves the opportunity to celebrate with you." Mrs. Dunham crossed her arms, battle stance ready.

"Am I not the one mated to the alpha?" Kristoff grumbled, the thought of a ceremonial hunt while not unappealing only served to bring about a frisson of fear. What if Jeremiah denied their bond? Refused the hunt? The way the man fucked him possessively each day, ensuring Kristoff bore his marks. The way he shared every possible moment with him and strove to involve Kristoff in all facets of his world should have solidified Kristoff's faith. Yet he was not without those times where that faith was a shallow brook and he the pebble that drifted along determined to find its way to Jeremiah's heart.

"Mated, yes. Bonded with the traditional ceremony, no. Your people agree that you are the alpha's mate, but a ceremony must occur, one for all to witness and herald in the leadership of the alpha pair."

"All of you got together and decided this?"

"Me and a few others." Her smile was a crafty one that gave Kristoff a few suspects to consider.

"So, is this your way of ensuring I don't leave?"

"Oh, no, my young one."

And that was funny seeing as Kristoff was over 100 years old, but Mrs. Dunham was older and perhaps more knowledgeable than he in some things.

"No, I don't feel you'll be going anywhere. Alpha's not going to make that mistake again. No, keeping you here is not the point, *a chroí*." *My heart.* The words made him smile. "The true desire is to honor the future and the growth of our pack. It's to celebrate the good that continues to thrive no matter the trials we have endured and the losses we have suffered. You, son, are a gift to us, and we ask to share in our alpha's happiness."

Mrs. Dunham waited for his response with her expression soft and the warmth in her eyes calming Kristoff's racing heart. He'd do anything for this woman who loved him without fail, had soothed him when he thought his heart would shatter in a million pieces, and who was there when he needed someone. Even now, she stood in the gap between

Kristoff and the other mother of his heart. Bringing Mrs. Hilliard to him, aiding him in rebuilding a relationship Kristoff thought he would have to do without. For Mrs. Dunham, Kristoff would even challenge his fears.

"Yes."

"There you are, darling. That's the infamous assassin I know and love. I knew you could do it."

"Betting was involved, wasn't there?"

"Oh, nary a thought. Only a few duckies that."

Kristoff smiled and drank his tea.

CHAPTER EIGHTEEN

Jeremiah smelled cinnamon and vanilla, the tantalizing scent stronger as he fucked his mate hard and deep. The taste of Kristoff's blood was enticing, the pleasure making his thrusts stutter. Kristoff had said yes.

"Fuck, Jeremiah," Kristoff growled when Jeremiah shoved his right thigh up over the desk, his pale skin begging to be marked by Jeremiah's palm. "You only had to ask. You didn't have to send Mrs. Dunham in here to do your dirty work."

"No, you're right about that, my love, but her way was so much better, and a great deal shorter."

Jeremiah punctuated his words with his thrusts before he wrapped himself around the large body of his mate. He gripped Kristoff's sweet ass tightly as he plunged into his welcoming heat.

"Perhaps." Kristoff gasped before shouting, "Deeper, my alpha."

"Whatever pleases you, my mate." Jeremiah complied with his mate's demands as he claimed Kristoff's throat, his canines sinking deep into his flesh.

Kristoff howled and rocked his ass back to take in Jeremiah's cock, over and over, riding him hard.

Their bodies, slick with sweat, slid back and forth on Kristoff's desk, his dick tracking a sticky path across the surface. Their heat built as Jeremiah took his mate, smiling when the extended claws of their clasped hands drew furrows in the wood's surface.

Being inside Kristoff was bliss, the sweet combination of

their entwined forms too tempting not to savor, to indulge in again and again.

"Love you so much, Kristoff. Need you, *agra*."

"And I, you."

The tingling of Jeremiah's orgasm broiled within, and he knew it would be mere moments before his seed erupted from his cock. He buried himself deep within Kristoff, the scent of their arousal and the wildness of their fucking so visceral yet tender. They exploded together.

Jeremiah held Kristoff against him as their heart rates settled and calmed. He placed gentle kisses along Kristoff's brow, scenting him, his wolf appeased for the moment. It wasn't enough, though. Not yet.

But soon it would be.

Soon Kristoff would be Jeremiah's in every way. Not only as a viable partner who aided Jeremiah as they led their people but as his alpha mate, his bonded mate. He would claim him before the pack. He would hunt Kristoff, and show his mate how much he needed him, how his wolf demanded his capture, his total and utter submission.

That night, Jeremiah held a sleeping Kristoff in his arms as he thought about how much easier life had become with his mate beside him. They'd been together before as alpha and beta, Kristoff in the role of Second, his arm ever ready to fight at Jeremiah's side.

Jeremiah wanted more than Kristoff's arm in battle, his icy countenance striking fear into Jeremiah's enemies. No, Jeremiah was alpha for a reason, his ability to fight and protect his people, his pack, was without question.

Jeremiah wanted all of Kristoff, his very soul, his freedom, to possess him entirely in a way Kristoff would respect. The same pack that sent Kristoff to Jeremiah years ago would respect the ceremonial hunt of the Iroquois Pack. The claim would be enough that Kristoff would no longer be used as a weapon, would not be pulled from the pack when needed. He would be the alpha's mate and remain beside him.

And it would please Jeremiah and his wolf tremendously for their mate to never leave their side again.

They stood in the forest, the glow of the Goddess Moon shining down on them.

Jeremiah roared, his human cry transitioning into his wolf's howl as bones cracked and tendons pulled until he stood on all fours. His massive body covered in the dense blue and black pelt that those around him recognized as alpha.

He breathed deep, inhaling the scent of his pack. He watched as they changed from their human forms to that of their wolves and joined his cry. His joy of the hunt echoing in their undulating howls.

Mate.

Mate.

Mate.

The word repeated through his mind, the single point of his focus.

Mate.

Jeremiah pawed the ground, ready to fly off into the wood and give chase, but he had to be patient. He had to wait.

His pack paced, nervous energy rampant as they waited to follow his lead, to aide him in the claiming of his mate.

His pack. His mate's pack.

Never would he be alone again.

Jeremiah spun, sniffing the air, his ears perking up, seeking out the slightest sound that gave away his mate's location.

He felt his mate, their souls entwined, calling for each other over the distance. But this had to be his mate's choice, Kristoff's decision.

He waited, backing up and knocking against the wolves

standing close. He welcomed the rubs against his side, the encouragement.

Trust.

Wait.

Trust.

And then he heard it. The howl of his mate, far off, perhaps miles away.

His mate issued the challenge.

Find me.

Claim me.

Possess me.

And Jeremiah's wolf tore across the earth, his pack behind him as they hunted the alpha's mate.

Kristoff's wolf cried loud, his howl bellowing across miles, ready for his mate to earn his fidelity. He turned then, speeding across uneven land, thundering over wet leaves, the caress of the Goddess Moon kissing the silvery pelt of his wolf.

His breaths were harsh as he ran, speeding away, refusing to give quarter to his alpha.

If he wanted him, he would show he was worthy.

If the pack needed him, they would aid the alpha in the capture of the alpha's mate.

His soul craved its mate, struggled with the distance between them, but he would not give in. He would fight, show that he, too, was worthy of the alpha's claim.

He ran.

Jeremiah's wolf knew his mate was near. It was quiet, too quiet. No creatures stirred, too afraid of drawing the predators' attention.

He opened his maw to taste the air and angled his head forward. The russet wolf beside him chuffed and circled around, his goal to corner the alpha mate.

Jeremiah then signaled the russet wolf's twin to take the other side while the youngest of his pack circled around back.

Jeremiah's muscles tensed, his eagerness to claim what belonged to him sending waves of arousal into the air.

They closed in, intent on the spot where his mate had camouflaged himself within the trees.

Heads lowered, they scented the alpha mate and closed in, Jeremiah taking the lead to claim as was his due.

Suddenly, the scent of wrongness assaulting him.

Something pierced him, sharp and wicked, then another, and another.

He was being shot.

All around him, wolves cried out in pain, the scent of blood heavy in the air.

Mate, he felt his mate call, worry dancing along their line.

No. Stay. Danger.

Jeremiah had to protect his mate. He couldn't allow what was befalling them to touch his mate.

No.

Mate. Protect.

The thoughts proceeded the movement of silvery fur Jeremiah knew as Kristoff's as he tore from his hiding place, ready to rip into the enemy.

"This is for you, Kristoff. You. We've been waiting for the right time," a voice shouted above the roars and confusion.

The enemy.

Jeremiah gasped as another bullet hit his already weakening frame. He refused to fall, though. His mate was in danger.

Protect. Shield. Love.

Jeremiah used his own healing to push the bullets from his flesh and turned to face the enemy.

A man stood, tall and thick, gun in hand. He wasn't alone. There were wolves with him, wolves that smelled wrong. Smelled broken. Tainted.

"You don't need to listen to anyone anymore. It took me years to figure out why you let me live, why you just didn't kill me. I waited. And then one day, I met someone, someone who knew about monsters, who knew you. And here I am, ready to give you your own pack, make you an alpha, lead with you. We just have to kill this one, and you can have the good ones that are left. Mix them in with the ones I brought with me. They were adrift and needed a leader. I promised them you. You and me, Kristoff. I'll even fuck you. I didn't like ass before, but a hole's a hole. I can give you what you need. All of it."

Jeremiah just needed to get close enough to tear out the man's throat. He shook away the pain, determined.

His mate growled dangerously, and Jeremiah could sense Kristoff was ready to attack but hesitated, afraid the human would shoot again.

Kristoff stepped forward, and the human raised his hand, a second gun pointed at Jeremiah.

Before he could get a shot off, Kristoff was on him, his teeth at the enemy's throat, the scent of rage rippling across the air to Jeremiah.

Chaos erupted, and the pack attacked, bloody and torn, but healing as they ripped away at the tainted wolves. Jeremiah would not be kept from the battle, no matter how his mate pushed at their connection.

Safe. Back. The words slammed against his brain.

Alpha.

Then Kristoff turned, his focus on ridding the enemy of his weapon, casting it away with his hand still attached to it. Then he was on the man's chest, wicked sharp canines tearing into the body that danced on the ground while screaming in terror.

At the enemy's fall, the tainted wolves who weren't engaged in battle backed away and ran.

Jeremiah barked at his mate, who lifted his head covered in bits of gore and blood. Kristoff backed away then, his will subject to his mate's. Though Jeremiah felt the need to eviscerate what remained of the man who had threatened his mate, he kept his attention on Kristoff.

Jeremiah waited while Kristoff ambled to him and fell to the ground on his belly. Jeremiah bent to lick away the blood covering his mate, cleaning away bits left behind.

When his pack members were done with the enemy wolves left behind, some who had escaped and others who lay in a heap on the forest floor, he huffed and was pleased to see them drag away the body of the leader.

Kristoff's focus was on Jeremiah, though. His concern clear.

Safe. Whole. Finish?

Jeremiah brushed his face against Kristoff's, nuzzling him, swiping his tongue over him tenderly.

Then he draped himself over his mate, satisfied with just the touch and the nearness of his form rather than taking him for all to see.

Others fell against them then, covering them both, sheltering them, licking their fur, and nipping at them.

Good. Good. Love. Welcome. Ours.

The sense of home and acceptance radiated among them all, and Kristoff accepted the claiming of the pack.

He was Jeremiah's.

He was theirs.

They were his.

EPILOGUE

Life without a mission was not a life Kristoff ever saw himself having, but he was fine. His most recent *mission* had consisted of curbing the appetite of a wayward Samuel, who had finally settled when Darren returned home. Order restored. And now, rather than the threat of an orgy, Samuel was going to class and finishing his nursing degree.

All was right in the world.

At least for now.

Jeremiah had healed from Stefan's attack, and Stefan was no more. As for the wolves that had arrived with the deluded human, they had disappeared. Conner was rounding them up and working on a treatment for the tainted ones. They posed a danger not only to themselves but also from their cooperation with Stefan. Lives had been lost and the innocent broken. They needed help, and Jeremiah was an alpha that believed in no wolf being lost. So Conner would find them all, and they would do their best to help.

And if they couldn't be helped? Well, decisions would have to be made. And that was where Kristoff came in. Taking care of problems was what he did.

He glanced at his reflection in the mirror, admiring the cut of the suit he wore. Perfect.

"You are beautiful as always, my alpha mate," Jeremiah said, wrapping his arm around him from behind. He ran one hand reverently over Kristoff's military cut hair. "I wish you'd let this grow."

"You just want to use it as another grip to fuck me. And no

kisses. We have to leave."

Jeremiah laughed. "That is not the only reason, *agra*. And you can't expect me to be this close to you and not get my lips on your skin." He drew his tongue along Kristoff's neck and nipped at the cord there.

"So, you don't deny wanting to use my hair for a better hold?" Kristoff couldn't help the raspy need in the tone of his voice.

"Of course not. Having the great Kristoff Dumanovsky at my mercy is one of my greatest pleasures." Jeremiah bit down, making Kristoff groaned and lean back.

The kiss they shared was a sweet heat that flamed between them, causing Kristoff's dick to fill quickly.

"I wish we had more time," Kristoff grumbled, "but young Peter has returned with an even larger entourage than the one he took when he departed."

"Ah, and they will be seeking asylum?" It was less a question and more a confirmation.

"Yes. And, of course, you will grant it just as you have given Mrs. Hilliard a room of her own."

The woman had fallen in love with the compound and the people when she came to visit. She hadn't wanted to return with her daughter, so she'd been given a room in the main house where she could dote on the children and chat with the women. Mrs. Hilliard had made herself a place, and her happiness was a tangible thing.

As for Kristoff? He was able to keep the mother of his heart. It was another gift from his mate, one for which he'd been grateful.

It was even more of a home to him now.

"Of course, and not just because these are your nephew's people, but because it is the right thing to do." Jeremiah drew his hand along the expensive suit Kristoff wore, tugging at the buttons.

Kristoff turned in his arms, pulling him close. "Thank you for coming for me," he said. "Thank you for fighting for me."

"I had to. It took me a while to realize just how stupid I had been, but when you were no longer beside me, my world flipped on its axis." Jeremiah's blue eyes reflected a bit of vulnerability. "Never leave me again, Kristoff. I can't promise I won't become the monster people whisper about in those fairy tales meant to frighten human young."

Kristoff kissed his mate gently, wanting his commanding alpha back. "You won't have to, Jeremiah. Loving you is forever. No broken promises."

Jeremiah sighed, and a look of peace and contentment crossed his face. "You know, they say promises are meant to be broken," he teased.

Kristoff smiled. "Not this one, my mate. Not now. Not ever."

One more kiss couldn't hurt. Their love was here and now. The rest of the world could wait.

YOU MAY ALSO ENJOY THE FOLLOWING FROM eXTASY BOOKS:

Getting There
Deja Black

Excerpt

"What the fuck is that smell," a deep voice shouted through the house. Anthony's rumble shook the walls, his deep voice hard as granite crashing along with the sounds of dishes and pans being shoved around. "Smells like some funkiness my cat threw up. Lucas, get your ass in here."

Anthony, Lucas's younger brother, was not a small man. From the sound of his movements in the kitchen, he was making his presence known, loud and clear, as delicate plates and glasses met their demise.

"Humph! Don't need this shit anyway. Lucas, come here." It wasn't hard to recognize the clangs and pings of items other than food finding their way into Lucas's trashcan.

Lucas pulled the pillow over his head. He'd had enough. Just two days ago — on the day of his three-year anniversary — Ira not only left him, but Tommy had offered to teach him how to keep a man? No, he was staying under the covers, in the dark, where it was safe.

Footsteps thundered his way, his brother's gruff voice slicing through the silence. "Lucas!"

Lucas shoved himself further under the down pillow. He heard curtains sliding along rods, and saw light peeking around the corners of the soft cotton.

"Too dark in here. I know you heard me. I've got to get to work."

"So," Lucas mumbled when the glaring sun assaulted his eyes as the pillow was lifted from his head. He tried to turn over and hide his face away from the brightness, but a huge hand all but pulled him out of bed.

"Shower for you." Long fingers carded through his thick curls and held him close. "There now." Anthony's arms were strong, a shelter in the storm of Lucas's life.

"Myra?" Lucas questioned. He breathed in the safety of his brother, the spicy scent of Anthony's favorite cologne going a long way to soothe his trembling.

"Yep. Seems someone told someone who spoke to someone else who called Mom who called our little sister. Of course, Myra called me after she tried speaking to you, which was a fail when she could barely understand you. And, here I am. So, let's organize your shit and get you and me the fuck out of here. Clock's ticking."

"So. Go." Lucas made to move back to the bed only to be gripped tighter and dragged to his own shower, the scent of Mahogany Woods saturating the bathroom. The water stung his skin while hands rubbed over him, the loofah filled with scented suds. Lucas looked down, Anthony's corded arms twisting him this way and that before rinsing him off. A towel was tossed at him before he was dried off and pushed toward the bedroom.

"What the fuck is in this closet? They're barely your size, and damn if they look like anything you'd wear."

Lucas knew what Anthony saw. Club clothes, tiny scraps of fabric Ira insisted he wear on the nights they'd gone out for an evening of fun with Ira's friends. He'd given Ira every-thing, even his dignity, and had dressed like his lover's arm-slut at night to please him.

The only other clothes would be what he'd wear to class — ties, dress shirts, fitted slacks. Ira tried to make him into a per-son he could never be. Then, he'd left him for the real deal. He fell back toward the bed wanting to climb back into the sheets and forget it all.

"No, Lucas. Not happening. Here, I've found pants and a shirt. It will do for now. Let's go."

"Go? Where?" Lucas did not intend to go anywhere.

"Work. From what Myra said, you sounded like you'd given up. Figured that asshole and the twit who worked for you threw you for a loop. She said it was hard to understand your words when you sounded like a wet rat who'd drowned itself in a bottle of Riesling."

Oh, the conversation that felt more like a dream. And, while it hadn't been Riesling, it had been equally intoxicating. In fact, there should be a bottle or three of it laying on the floor around somewhere.

Lucas jumped when a phone buzzed somewhere. He hadn't plugged his phone back in last night, so it couldn't be his. Anthony pulled his cell out of his jean pocket. Dressed casually in a plaid shirt and a pair of jeans with flip flops, he didn't appear to be headed into work.

A police officer for the Charleston Police Department and former military, Anthony was professional, always. So, the fact he wasn't wearing his uniform spoke greatly to how con-cerned he was about his older brother, regardless of the calm façade he wore.

"Yeah." Anthony paused while the speaker on the other end of the phone continued. The voice sounded animated and high-pitched with worry. Myra. Of course, it could be their mother, Cassandra. The two sounded a great deal alike. "I got him. Taking him with me. Right. House smells like crap. He looks like it, too. Don't worry. I got it. He won't be alone.

Don't worry now. Go to class."

His youngest sister was in college now finishing up her second year studying to be a veterinarian. She'd always possessed a love for animals, so it was natural she wanted to care for them. A nurturer, Myra felt it was her duty to look out for those she loved, and apparently, Lucas was at the top of that list right now.

Heavy hands fell on his shoulders, worried dark green eyes searching his. "You seriously look like warmed over shit. But, it will have to do for now." Anthony lifted his ball cap, bent low and kissed Lucas on his cheek. "We'll get you sorted. Don't worry." Lucas noticed the handles of his Cole Haan overnight bag and his laptop case dwarfed in his younger brother's large hand.

"I don't want to go with you," Lucas pouted, his voice as weary and as exhausted as he felt.

"Not an option," Anthony said as he took Lucas's elbow to lead him out.

"I'm older than you," Lucas grumbled when a lightweight jacket was placed on his shoulders.

"Not arguing that," Anthony replied while he turned to lock the door. "But, you're mine, you're outnumbered, and the department is waiting. So, hop your ass in the truck, and we'll hash this out later."

Anthony massaged Lucas's shoulder as he and Lucas moved toward Anthony's monster vehicle on wheels, leaving the home he shared with Ira behind them.

ABOUT THE AUTHOR

Deja Black had fantasies of men loving men, men who felt strongly, loved hard and needed a hero. Then one great day she came across a book and discovered the world of m/m writing, encountered others who shared her obsession as much as she did, and found a world where she could not only be accepted for the lives and loves she envisioned, but she could create them too. So why not? Why not take the stories she would write and throw away as a teenager, grow them, dream them, and make them a reality where she could let them live their story, and make them real for someone else? And she did. Now, with the support of her hubby and some intense time management, she is learning to balance her family of two energetic children at home along with the many students she teaches every day as well as her passion of writing what she loves to read.

Deja is always interested in connecting to new people who also share her love, so please feel free to contact her at:
Facebook: www.facebook.com/deja.black.69
Blog: dejablack77.blogspot.com
Twitter: @DejaBlack69

www.ingramcontent.com/pod-product-compliance
Lightning Source LLC
Chambersburg PA
CBHW060617130626
46555CB00002B/549